# Surviving the Nahanni

W. A. Welsh

# DEDICATION

For Caleb

Never stop trying to improve yourself and never be afraid to take chances. Love and enjoy life.

# CHAPTER 1

"Dad, do you think the pool will be finished in time for my birthday party?"

Evan Keller had been able to think of nothing else since the family decided to install an in-ground pool at their modest home in rural upstate New York.

"I don't know buddy. It will take the contractors some time to dig the hole, set the walls and install the liner, and after that, the cement patio has to be poured. It's going to be close."

At this Evan let out a deep sigh, the way impatient eight-year-olds will do, and went back to eating his scrambled eggs. His father did not have the heart to tell his boy that it would be far too late in the year to swim by the time the pool was installed. After all, it was already the first of September.

Erik Keller had other things on his mind anyway. He was about to embark on the trip of a lifetime with his best friend. They would be leaving early the next morning on a long-awaited hunting and fishing trip in the great Canadian Northwest Territory. For weeks he had been nearly giddy with anticipation, like a child at Christmas.

The problem was that Erik was not a child; he was a 42-year-old man with a myriad of responsibilities and a wife who was not crazy about the timing of this trip.

"Honey, you know I'm happy for you, but this trip could not be happening at a worse time. The boys are starting school, things are getting busy at the University, the pool is going in.....and the money."

Lauren tucked a tuft of her blonde hair behind her ear as she busily scribbled on the calendar that hung on the refrigerator. She was right. This was not the best time to be leaving. Evan was starting third grade, Lauren's job as a professor at Syracuse University kept her busy and on the go. There was also the issue of Calvin.

The Keller's oldest son Calvin had just started

his sophomore year in college. The first year was tough for him academically, as well as being away from home for the first time. Over the summer his longtime girlfriend had broken up with him and he had been in an absolute funk all summer.

"I'll talk to Cal before I leave, dear. Kids go through these things, he'll be fine. And we've already discussed the money situation; I'll borrow from my retirement account to pay for the trip. I've got almost nine years left until retirement. It's plenty of time to catch up."

He did his best to soothe her worries and gently kissed Lauren on the forehead before placing his breakfast plate in the dishwasher.

"What time do you leave in the morning, Dad?" chirped Evan.

"Very early. Are you coming to the airport to see me and Uncle John off?"

"Mom, can I?" asked young Evan.

"If you can get your lazy butt out of bed we will see," Lauren said, smiling at her son.

She wished she could be his age and get as excited over such trivial things.

"Let's go, Evan. Your Mom has to go to work and we have some errands to run."

Erik's mind was a mix of excitement, worry, and anticipation. All of his gear and guns had been shipped ahead of time to Watson Lake in Canada's Northwest Territory. There were still last minute preparations to make though. Erik had to purchase some cold weather gear, double-check on some last minute shift swaps at work, stop at the post office and drop off a deposit to the contractor who was installing the swimming pool.

The guys at work seemed genuinely happy for him. Erik had been a corrections officer at Carter Correctional Facility in central New York for over fifteen years. It was a very rural area and most of his fellow officers were sportsmen as well. They knew how long he'd been waiting for this trip to come together and were very helpful with covering for him at work.

His job was extremely dangerous and stressful and aside from the love of his family to get him through, there was the dream of this great Canadian hunting adventure. When John called him to say that after more than twenty years of applying for the Canadian moose hunting lottery their numbers had finally been drawn, well Erik could hardly believe it.

Now the time was here. Tomorrow morning he would be leaving to fulfill a dream nearly thirty years in the making.

Yet, somehow he still felt guilty.

# Chapter 2

It was raining extremely hard when Lauren pulled her SUV up to the curb in front of Syracuse's Hancock Airport. Evan was already asleep in the backseat and the clock had not yet reached four AM. Erik and his wife both sat silently for a minute in the front seat of their blue Dodge Durango.

"I know this is bad timing, I'm sorry," Erik said, breaking the silence.

"I'll be back in nine days, I'll work some overtime. We will get back on top of things regarding the boys, I promise."

"Stop it already, everything is fine. We'll be O.K. What kind of wife would I be to deny you this? Everything will be fine, have fun. Tell John I said 'Good Luck'."

Lauren had her hair pulled back and there was still sleep in her eyes. She had a crease across her cheek from her pillow. Erik thought to himself that she was still as beautiful as the day he'd met her twenty years ago.

"I love you," she said.

"I love you too," Erik replied.

"Remember there is no cell service up there. You might not hear from me for several days. In the event of an emergency leave a message at the ranger station in Watson Lake. Goodbye honey, I'll miss you."

"Bye. Please be safe," she said softly, and with that he watched her pull away.

As he entered the airport and headed for the ticket counter he found himself missing his family already. Aside from Lauren's work trips for the University they had never spent more than four or five days apart. The same thing with the kids, he and Lauren has taken a few long weekends away before but never had he been away from the boys as long as he would be this time.

Erik decided that he would have to suspend his worries. Nothing should stand in the way of his full enjoyment of this long-awaited trip.

As he made his way through the ticket counter and through security he started to think of the nightmarish travel that lay ahead. The flight from Syracuse would take him to Denver. From there it was on to Juneau, then into Canada to Whitehorse. After that, it was a bush plane to Watson Lake and finally one last bush plane over the great Nahanni National Park Reserve to the small town of Deline on Great Bear Lake. With any luck, they would be in Deline and their rented lodge by midnight.

In all, they were looking at five flights and nearly a whole day of travel.

Once in the terminal, Erik started looking for his best friend. It wasn't hard to pick him out of the crowd with his camouflage hat and a huge smile.

"Are you ready buddy?" John beamed as he gave Erik a giant bro hug. It was apparent that Erik was not the only one filled with excitement and anticipation.

John Woodsley and Erik Keller met in the fifth grade during a spirited game of dodge ball on the school playground. Erik had plunked John in the nose and the ever hot-headed John charged him. The boys tumbled, wrestled and punched until their teacher, Mrs. Williamson, grabbed them both by the ears and sat them on the back stairs. They were both suspended from recess and forced to sit next to each other on those stairs for a whole week.

Over the course of that week, forced out of boredom to speak to each other, the two boys became best friends. They bonded over their love of the outdoors. After school, from fifth grade through the end of high school, they could be found in the woods and waterways of their rural hometown. They hunted and fished and talked of the day, when they were older and grown, that they could head to Alaska or Northern Canada to hunt bear and moose and fish the mighty lakes.

Now that day was here and the two inseparable pals were going to live out that dream.

Never had two best friends been more unalike. John was tall and lanky with a wisp of blonde hair, Erik was stocky, barely five foot eight and his dark hair was shaved close to his head. John was the last of six children, a late in life baby, and his parents were well off. Erik was the oldest of three and came from a lower middle class working family. When John went off to college,

Erik went to work. They had spent years apart at times but always kept in touch and never gave up on their dream.

Now, both 42 years old, fate had found them living in neighboring towns, although they still had different lives. Erik was a loyal family man and had his job at the prison. His life was filled with sports practices, trips to the dentist's office and family vacations. John was still a bachelor, although he had a ten-year-old daughter from a short relationship who he saw infrequently. He taught history at Wolcott High School and coached the baseball team. He still dated various women and traveled in the summer.

Both men secretly envied the other at times.

"Are you ready for all of this shitty travel?" asked John.

"I'm not looking forward to it but I know once we are in the Territory we're gonna love it," Erik replied.

With a nod, John agreed.

It was John who did the vast majority of the leg work for this trip. He had rented the lodge and secured the guide in Deline. He was the one who spent weeks aligning flights, matching up arrivals and departures to save as much time as possible. Lastly, it was John who, every year for twenty years without fail, devotedly applied for the Canadian moose hunting lottery to win permits. When John called Erik with news that they had finally won those permits he was so thrilled he could barely speak.

The two men's minds raced as they boarded the 4:45 AM plane bound for Denver, their childhood dreams about to come true.

# Chapter 3

Approximately ten hours later the men were in Juneau about to leave on a much smaller plane for Whitehorse, Canada. The trip so far had gone rather pleasantly and Erik had spent most of his time either sleeping or reading Canadian travelogues. John, who was in charge of the travel arrangements, preferred to sip whiskey and watch movies. He deferred all the details of the country, terrain and hunt to Erik.

From the time Erik was very small he was a list maker and planner. Organization and preparedness were actually enjoyable to him. It was one of the reasons that Lauren, who had a Ph.D. in Business and Organizational Management, loved him so much. Every Keller vacation since Calvin was in diapers was researched, studied and prepared for as if there would be a test given before they could leave.

John knew that Erik had studied the history of Canada's Northwest and Yukon Territories. He knew every mountain, lake, and river within 100 miles of where they would be staying. Erik had also read every rule and law regarding fishing and hunting seasons, memorized average rainfalls and temperatures, even the times of the sunrise and sunset.

Both men were confident that they were well prepared. All of the proper rifles and rods were purchased, all types of climate-appropriate clothes have been packed. They had waited so long for this trip and they did not want unpreparedness to stand in the way of the trip of a lifetime.

They switched planes in Whitehorse and boarded a small plane to Watson Lake. It would be their final stop in the Yukon before flying into the Northwest Territories. There were only the pilot, John and Erik and an older couple who were going to visit their son who was working in the area. By now the sun was getting near the horizon and the men hoped to be in the air on the last leg of their journey by sundown. Erik and John marveled as they looked out the window at the splendor below, for what they saw was the stuff of their dreams.

They were now over the Yukon wilderness and the view was incredible. Nothing as far as the eyes could see but stands of pine and fir, mountain tops, rivers, and lakes. The greens and the blues were brighter and more vivid than either man had ever imagined.

"Wow," John said softly, his voice barely above a whisper. "You can't see a road or town anywhere."

Erik agreed, "I can't believe how remote it is."

Before the men knew it the plane was touching down in Watson Lake on a tiny landing strip next to a small hangar.

"That's your plane over there, the yellow one. Grab your bags guys," their pilot instructed them.

As Erik and John approached the yellow plane a short, dirty looking man who looked to be in his mid-fifties appeared.

"You Woodsley?" the man asked John.

"Yes sir," John replied.

"I'm Gus Atkins, I'll be flyin' you two to Deline. Now get your shit in the plane, I don't like takin' off after dark."

John and Erik were a little taken aback by the man's direct language, but this was a rough country and this guy could definitely be described as 'rough'. They shared a chuckle.

"I made arrangements for our equipment to be delivered here," John directed at Gus.

"Yeah, I know. It's all on a pallet over by the plane. I'm not gonna load it for you. Get it all in the back of the tail and make sure it's all secured with the cargo net. I'm going to get some coffee, and then I'll take you two to Deline. That's all I'm gettin' paid for."

"This guy's got a million-dollar personality, 'eh?" Erik whispered to John.

Laughing the old curmudgeon off, the two men started to load their gear into the back of the plane. They had sent plenty of gear to Watson Lake and for the first time they wondered if they'd overdone it. There were rifles, ammo, tents, fishing gear, and rods. There were sleeping bags, cold-weather gear and several pairs of boots. Erik had even packed several maps and a GPS device.

Eric found his .40 caliber model 23 Glock, his favorite handgun, and decided to place it in its holster and carry it on his hip. It made him feel manly and he wanted to really play the part of the 'rugged outdoorsman'.

"I've got a surprise for you," John said. With that, he produced THE bottle.

"No shit, you're kidding me!" exclaimed Erik.

In John's hand was a 30-year-old bottle of Canadian Mist whiskey. When the two were twelve years old they had stolen it from John's father's liquor cabinet. They had dared each other to take a drink but were both too scared. It was John that came up with the idea of saving it for their future hunting trip. The bottle was old and the label faded and peeling.

"Thirty years ago we swore we'd drink this whole bottle after we kill a moose," John beamed, "I didn't forget buddy."

Erik let out a hearty laugh, "Alright my man! That bottles coming back empty, a promise is a promise."

They laughed as they finished packing the plane.

# Chapter 4

"Alright, you city boys ready to fly?" snarled Gus. "You two are in for a treat today, this plane is the best in the sky and you got the best pilot."

Erik and John rolled their eyes at each other at the reference to them as 'city boys'. They spent more time in the woods than anyone they knew and had grown up in a rural farming community. But, Gus was right about one thing, the little yellow plane was a beauty.

"What kind of plane is this?" asked John.

"The best kind. It's a Murphy Moose. Built right here in Canada in 2011. It'll do 175 kmh and fly at 15,000 ft. It only needs 600 feet of runway to get her airborne. They only built a couple of hundred, but I know a guy so I got mine first. Everybody in the Territories knows the name, Gus

Atkins."

Gus's chest thumping and annoying attitude were already wearing thin on the men.

"Jesus, this guys an asshole," John whispered to Erik.

"I know, and he's sweating like he just ran a marathon. His eyes look weird. Reminds me of inmates in the prison when they're high on drugs."

The prop began to spin as the engine roared to life.

"Let's get going, I told you I don't like takin' off after dark!" Gus roared.

The men looked at each other and shrugged. They boarded the plane and buckled up next to each other. As the plane approached the runway Erik couldn't help but see how short it was, but the Murphy Moose lived up to Gus's word and accelerated quickly and both men let out a relaxed breath as the wheels departed from the ground.

The plane was slightly larger than most bush planes Erik had read about. It was over 20 feet long and could seat four passengers plus the pilot. The back row was folded down and the tail section was filled with all of the men's gear which was secured with a cargo net attached to the walls. Small planes like this did not react well to heavy shifting loads.

"I'm gonna take a slightly more northern route than I normally would gotta show you boys something before we lose light," Gus said through the headsets that all three men were now wearing.

"It's not going to make us late is it?" inquired John.

The men were tired and it had been a long day of traveling. They still had to meet their guide and get to their lodge. Not to mention both men were starving.

"Relax. It's only a couple minutes outta the way."

The sun was now low on the horizon and the skyline was a beautiful orange and blue. Again, Erik and John were mesmerized by the natural beauty that passed below them.

After a few moments Gus spoke, "There it is the town of Tungsten. I was a big shot foreman there in the early two-thousands. Before the goddamn corporations closed us down. Everybody down there knew me."

"Is it called Tungsten because that's what they

mined?" asked John.

"Uhh, yeah. You're a quick one. Why else would they call it that?" cracked Gus.

He laughed obnoxiously and Erik could see the anger on John's face. Erik shot John a quick look that said '*Don't let this idiot get to you*'.

Erik had read about the Tungsten mines. They were open pit mines and at one time half of the world's tungsten came from there. They were nestled in the Mackenzie Mountains, which were really just a northern extension of the American Rocky Mountains and the range ran all the way through this area. Erik also knew they were crossing the border out of the Yukon and into the Northwest Territories. The next stop, about ninety minutes away, was Deline and the hunt of a lifetime. Erik also knew they were about to cross over the Great Canadian Nahanni National Park Reserve, of which he'd read extensively. Too bad it was dark now and he wouldn't be able to see it from the sky.

Oh well, he thought. Maybe he'd see it on the return trip.

# Chapter 5

Erik waved in and out of sleep for the next forty-five minutes or so. He knew it must be after 9 pm in their time zone because his smartphone said the sunset at Watson Lake was slightly after eight. The hum of the engine was soothing and except for the glow of the instrument panel, there was little light. Even Gus had managed shut his yapper for awhile. Erik drifted off again.

"Erik!! Erik, get up NOW!" John screamed.

Erik leaped from his seat and tried to clear his brain.

"Gus is having a heart attack or something!!" John said as he reached for the pilot.

Gus was coughing and his face was beet red, Erik could see the panic in eyes by the dim light.

"Gus, are you alright, do you need something?

If you can speak say something," both men yelled.

Time seemed to slow down to Erik as he continued to yell, and eventually, he saw Gus slump over to his right. He couldn't quite believe what was happening but John's voice brought him back to reality.

"Erik! Help me get him out of this seat."

Both men quickly pulled Gus's lifeless body from the pilot's seat and lay him in on the floor in front of the seats they had been sitting in moments before. It was very close quarters and the men banged off the sides and ceiling off the plane as they did their best not to panic.

John sat in the pilot seat and started looking around as he placed one hand on the yoke, "Erik get on the radio and give a distress call!!!"

Erik fumbled with the plane's radio as he tried to find Gus's headset, "John try to find the artificial horizon gauge, you've got to keep the plane level!!"

"Yeah, yeah. I got it, I got it. I need to find the damn altimeter; I don't know how high we are!!!!"

Erik quickly changed the radio dial, staying on no frequency for more than a few seconds, "Mayday, mayday. A plane leaving Watson Lake, pilot dead. Need help to land. Repeat we need assistance!!"

Erik chanted out the same line repeatedly as he flew through the channels. It seemed like forever since Gus had lost consciousness but Erik knew it had only been a minute at most.

"Try doing some chest compressions on him Erik," John screamed, "I can't see anything but darkness and I sure as hell can't land this thing!"

Erik pressed his ear to the old pilot's chest and heard nothing. Regardless, he began pushing up and down in Gus's chest. He'd had training at work and knew what to do, but this situation was critical and he found himself trying to help John more than Gus, whom he believed was already dead anyway.

"John, how's it going? Tell me something. Please!!"

"I can't find the fucking altimeter anywhere!!" John screamed, real panic in his voice.

"I'm going to decelerate and try to see if I can see the ground, maybe it'll help us get our bearings," John pronounced.

Erik could hear the propellers slow as John pulled back on the throttle.

"I don't think that's a good idea, this is rough country, there's nowhere flat," Erik argued.

"Yeah, for all I know we are about to hit a mountain so do me a favor and buckle up and get on that radio again."

Erik found the headset again, left the radio on channel nine and buckled himself into his seat. Luckily the cord on the dead pilot's headset reached all the way back. He began his Mayday call again.

"Mayday!! Mayday!! We've just left Watson… John, I can see something. What is that?"

"I can see it too, its……Shit!!! Hold on!!!" John yelled.

Erik felt the plane jolt violently upward and to the left as he saw John pull back hard on the yoke.

"JOHN !!!!" Erik could hear himself scream.

The last thing he heard was the sound of breaking glass and scraping metal.

# Chapter 6

It was raining heavily.

This was the first conscious memory Erik Keller had. He was groggy and pain was shooting through his entire being. Wet salty blood filled his mouth. Lying on his left side he tried to make some sense of where he was. Confusion and pain were the only constants.

Surrounded by complete darkness, he could hear the rain but for some reason, he was not getting wet.

*What the hell is going on*, Erik thought to himself.

The sound of the rain drown out all of his senses, there was no up or down. There were no smells and certainly no other noises. There were just pain and rain.

Erik slowly lost consciousness again.

Warm sun on his face was how he was awakened for the second time and this time his senses were on fire. The smell of acrid smoke hung heavy in the air. He felt abounding pain everywhere in his body, primarily his head and left arm. He lifted his head, fighting the urge to vomit, and could see what appeared to be large rocks.

This time Erik knew exactly where he was and what had happened.

He was lying in the wreckage of a plane that had gone down the night before. Surprisingly, Erik did not feel panic, at least not right away.

*Get yourself out of this plane*, Erik's brain was telling him.

Slowly he reached for his seatbelt, using his right hand as his left was trapped under his own body weight. He had been lying on his side for some time and fumbled as he tried to regain the feeling and use of his extremities. Finding the buckle release he pressed down, as he did he realized that the belt was the only thing keeping him attached to the wreckage. Erik instantly barrel rolled to his left and pain shot through his body. He landed on the cold ground covered with small stones and with a great deal of effort he pulled himself to a seated position.

He was looking directly at the side of what was left of the yellow Murphy Moose. Erik pulled himself to his feet and stumbled back a few yards from the wreckage. His right pant leg was soaked in blood and as he turned behind himself he saw nothing but mountain peaks, ridges, and low lying clouds. Far below he could make out valleys and what appeared to be stands of pine and spruce. One thing was for sure, he was at a very high elevation.

Turning back towards the wreckage Erik wondered to himself how he was even alive. Before him, all that was left of the Moose was part of its left wing and its tail section. The only part of the body of the plane that was left was the floor, the seat where he was sitting and a small piece of sheet metal that had once been part of the roof. It was as if the plane had been sliced in half, diagonally, from front to back.

Black smoke, like that of a long-ago extinguished campfire, slowly rose from behind the wreckage. Small pieces of metal, cloth, gear, and machinery covered the ground. The smell of burnt fuel filled the air.

Again, Erik looked in both directions. The sun was warm on the back of his neck.

"I'm screwed," he murmured to himself.

He sat back down on a large rock and tried to clear his mind.

# Chapter 7

The best Erik could tell it was mid-morning. He searched his pants pocket for his smartphone, there would be no signal out here but at least he could see what time it was. The phone was nowhere to be found, just loose change and a small pocket knife remained in his pocket. Erik was happy and surprised to find his trusty Glock still holstered upon his hip.

*Where is John*, he thought to himself. He began to realize that if he was alive, his best friend may be as well. Furthermore, he may be hurt seriously and need help.

"JOHN!!! WOODSLEY!!!! CAN YOU HEAR ME!!! "

Erik's throat was dry and raspy as he yelled

out. His chest hurt with every deep breath. He repeated his call a couple more times. There was no response other than the eerie echo of his voice rattling off the mountainside. The other half of the plane was nowhere in sight and neither was his friend or the pilot.

*Should I climb around and search some of these ledges?*

It would be beyond foolish at this moment, he decided. He was hurt, he knew it. It was time to take stock of his physical condition. Sitting down on the same rock as he had before, Erik inspected his body.

A large cut was on his right forehead at the hairline. It was an open wound, still sticky with blood. The left side of his chest and ribcage hurt when he breathed and it was obvious that there were a few bruised or broken ribs. Inspecting the inside of his mouth he found that he must have bitten the inside of his cheek and had a couple of loose teeth on the top left. This accounted for disgusting blood taste in his mouth.

A deep worrisome gash ran vertically down his right shin. It was still bleeding and needed to be wrapped as soon as possible. Perhaps worst of all Erik's left hand was grotesquely swollen and discolored. Some of the bones in his hand and at least his two outer fingers were broken. His hand had been crushed on impact.

Stumbling back to the plane he was determined to find some cloth for wrapping his cuts and with any luck some medical supplies.

*Gus must have had a first aid kit.*

His only worry was trying to treat himself and find his friend. There was no place in his mind or heart for concern about Gus. That old fool was at fault, probably unfit to be flying in the first place. Erik found himself becoming angry at the man.

Shaking his head and getting himself back on point he continued to circle the wreckage. Peering into the tail section he saw that the cargo netting had ripped and most of the gear was missing. Ironically, amongst all the wreckage, there was nothing in the immediate sight of any use. Rubber, cloth and metal fragments were strewn about.

Erik realized, as he searched, that he was super lucky that he had no broken bones in his feet or legs. Plenty of bruising, scrapes and cuts, but no signs of anything serious on his lower body other than the deep cut. Continuing on, past the tail, he saw his first sign of any hope.

Resting against a boulder was a blue backpack. It must have belonged to John or Gus because he didn't recognize it as his own. Plopping down beside it he quickly worked the zipper and looked inside.

The bag was filled with undergarments and several pairs of tube socks. A bottle of cholesterol medicine, prescribed to one John Woodsley of Wolcott, New York, let Erik know whose bag it was. He was amused by the gaudy colors of his friend's boxer briefs. At the bottom of the bag, he found a full bottle of Poland Spring water and a granola bar.

He opened the bottle and drank greedily. The water was warm but refreshing and Erik was glad to wash the blood from his mouth. Saving half of the bottle, he put it to the side. Tearing open his pant leg Erik tied several pairs of tube socks around his injured shin. His injured left hand made it difficult and it took him many attempts.

*This should at least stop the bleeding.*

Using his pocket knife, he shredded another tube sock lengthwise, and tied it around his forehead wound, wearing it like a bandana. He placed the half bottle of water into the backpack, picked it up and circled the plane some more. Among his findings were a damaged fishing tackle box, a badly torn sleeping bag and a plastic bag with two dark green raincoats inside.

He placed the items in a pile and sat back down on what now was becoming his favorite rock. His head was pounding and he knew he needed some rest before he could search any further. His body was exhausted and he likely had a concussion. Nausea was overwhelming him, overpowering his fear and concern.

Erik spread the sleeping bag out in front of his sitting rock, took another sip of water and lay down on his back.

*I wonder if they realize our plane hasn't arrived in Deline yet. I hope Lauren and the boys don't know anything yet,* his mind raced.

He made an effort to slow his breathing and tried best he could to relax his tense muscles. Resting on his back he stared at the clear Canadian sky. He saw no birds, no planes, no clouds. Only the brightness of the midday sun, which made him close his eyes.

Once again he was out cold. Injury, fear, and exhaustion had forced his body to rest.

# Chapter 8

Erik Keller awoke on his back staring at the sky, the same way he'd fallen asleep. There was no way of telling what time it was. With much pain, he rose and sat again on his rock. It was getting chilly and Erik knew it would be dark soon. From where the sun was setting in the west he had gained his first piece of valuable information. He must be on the Northwest side of whatever mountain or ridge he was stranded on.

Everything he had ever read about these kinds of disaster scenarios said the same thing. Stay in one place, it gives searchers the best chance to find you. This was fine but perhaps not in this scenario, Erik thought to himself.

First of all, he was at a great elevation. Would planes even be able to fly over and see down through what would be cloud cover a great deal of the time?

Due to his extensive research, Erik knew he was somewhere in the Mackenzie Mountain range and surely no searchers would come up here on foot, at least not without a definite target and decent climbing equipment. Nobody was going to wander by, that was for damn sure.

Secondly, sitting and waiting for someone else was certainly not in his set of character traits. Lauren often told him he was the most impatient person she'd ever known.

After a short time, he had decided on a plan, one that he knew damn well could have his life depending on it. He would continue to search for supplies and more importantly, John. He would spend one night here at the wreckage site and tomorrow he would pack and try to head down to lower elevations. From there he would try to find the streams, rivers or roads that would take him to civilization.

The plan sounded simple in his head. But he knew better.

This country was as wild and untamed as it got. Some considered the Yukon to be on par with the Amazon as the last great unsettled areas on Earth. Erik had no way of knowing if he could even climb down, let alone conquer the other hazards. Starvation, infection, freezing cold temperatures, and even predators lived below. Add perhaps the roughest terrain known to man and maybe his plan was stupid.

Erik decided to start his search and stop worrying about things he couldn't control. Slowly, he made his way past the tail section and through the maze of boulders. He tried to keep his eyes open for anything he might find useful later on.

About one hundred yards past the tail section, to the east, he was stopped by a sheer wall of stone. To the right of the wall was a steep drop, one he could never manage to descend. He looked over the edge, perhaps three hundred feet down, and saw more of the same. Impassable ledges and stone as far as the eye could see.

Walking west past the wreckage was more of the same. The ridge on which Erik and the wreckage sat was perhaps two hundred yards long and came away from the mountain less than fifty. To go down, the only route Erik could see was the steep slope to the northwest that he had spied when he first exited the damaged craft. Far below was the only place he could see trees, perhaps miles down. Where there were trees there was shelter, a way to escape the wind and elements.

Although it had been relatively calm up there so far, Erik knew it wouldn't stay that way for long. The further down he went it was bound to be warmer too, at least he hoped. Finding water, which he needed more than anything, also depended on his traversing downwards.

It had been, he guessed, hovering around the mid-fifties in temperature all day. But while researching his trip Erik knew it had been an unusually cold summer and was it was now approaching autumn. The average temperature was highs of about 45 and lows in the twenties this time of year. Rain, wind and darkened valleys where the sun didn't shine could be deadly.

Erik remained dressed in the same clothes he had worn since the beginning of his trip. Hunting boots, blue jeans, a t-shirt covered with a flannel shirt and a light jacket were all he had to protect him from the cold and wind.

As Erik looked up all he could see was the face of the mountain that imprisoned him. He could see no other wreckage or sign of life. John Woodsley was the best friend he'd ever had or ever would have. He didn't want to give up on his friend, but what could he do? There was a sheer mountain face above him and he knew he must be within a few hundred feet of the peak. Below him, there was no wreckage. If the other half of the plane was nearby it was definitely not reachable.

Erik was caught off guard by a wave of emotion and he softly began to cry, he would have to leave this place without John. He knew there was no other choice, still, he felt ashamed. His body was tired and broken and he could never climb upwards. This didn't matter. His friend was most likely dead, and he realized this, but it still felt as though he was abandoning a brother.

After a few moments, he pulled himself together and continued to scour the area. It was near completely dark when he arrived back to the wreckage and the 'sitting rock'. He had managed to find more socks, a mostly used roll of duct tape, a magazine about planes, about fifty feet of paracord and a half pack of cigarettes. The pack must have belonged to Gus as neither Erik nor John smoked. Inside was a Bic lighter, maybe the best of Erik's haul. He kept the lighter and tossed the smokes.

Tomorrow, Erik decided, he would build some sort of sled to pull behind him. It would hold what few treasures he had found. Then he would head down the mountain. What happened after that was anybody's guess, but he damn sure wasn't going to die up here feeling sorry for himself.

Erik grabbed the torn sleeping bag, climbed into the tail section of the old Moose and hunkered down, determined to stay out of the rapidly dropping temperatures.

# Chapter 9

"Mom, do you think Dad shot a moose yet? I hope he texts me some pictures when he does," inquired Evan to his Mother.

"Honey, I told you. There is very little cell service up there, we might not hear from Dad for quite a while. Besides, he's only been gone a couple of days. Uncle John said sometimes people hunt for two weeks and never even see a moose up there."

It was early on a weekend morning and Lauren's brain was headed in several different directions. She and Evan were on their way to the mall in Syracuse to do some school clothes shopping. The contractors were starting to dig the hole for the pool today, and she was distracted by the meeting she would have Monday with several students at the University for a project that they were working on.

Of all the things on her mind at the top was her worry for her son Calvin who was starting his sophomore year at college. The previous year had been an extreme challenge for him academically and Lauren could tell he was not looking forward to returning. Calvin had been moping around the house all summer and had broken up with his longtime girlfriend from high school. He was becoming a man and going through some grown-up obstacles.

Lauren had done her best to give him space but was constantly being reminded by Erik that, 'kids go through these things and you have to let them figure it out on their own.' She knew it was true but it did nothing to calm her maternal worries.

"There's a parking spot, Mom," Evan chirped from his passenger's side seat.

As much as Calvin worried her, Evan did the opposite. She looked at him with his sandy blonde hair and cherub cheeks and marveled at what he was. He was all 'boy,' innocent and naturally happy, and was an absolute joy to have in the house. Aside from occasional whining about not being able to do what his older brother was allowed to do, she had no problems with him. She admired his perpetual cheeriness and his genuine friendliness to just about everybody he met.

The other three members of the Keller household were prone to moodiness and sulking, it was Evan who kept a measure of silliness and sunshine in their lives.

"Mom, when I get older I'm gonna go to Alaska with Dad and Uncle John."

"Oh? What about Calvin?"

"He won't wanna go, he's not into outdoors stuff like we are."

By now they were in a clothing store and she was sizing up Evan for some pants.

"Come here, I want you to try these on."

"Awww Mom, nobody wears jeans to school. Just athletic shorts and sweatshirts," her young man complained.

"I don't care what other people wear. You're not wearing shorts to school in the middle of a central New York winter."

With that young Evan took his jeans into the

changing room. Lauren was in the footwear aisle waiting for Evan to come out when she received the call. Her phone chirped in her spring robin ringtone as she reached in her purse to answer it.

"Hello?"

"Hello. Is this Lauren Keller of 358 Lilly Lane?"

"Yes, who's this?" She prepared to hang up on what she thought was a telemarketer.

"Ma'am, this is Lt. Ron Jenkins of the Royal Canadian Mounted Police. I'm calling from our Watson Lake detachment. Ma'am, we've received word from both Lemiure outfitters in Deline and the Deline airport manager that your husband's flight never arrived yesterday."

"How can that be? Maybe they decided to drive the last leg of the trip or they stayed over an extra night?" she replied as she could feel her heart begin to beat faster.

"Ma'am we've thought of that too. The problem is this .......several people at the Watson Lake air terminal watched your husband and his traveling companion leave. A local pilot in the area was flying them to Deline and Ma'am,..... he and his plane are unaccounted for as well."

Lauren stood silent for a moment, unable to process what she was hearing. Her phone was still to her ear but she was unable to speak.

"Mom, how do these look? They feel tight," asked Evan who was now standing by her side.

"Ma'am??......Are you still there?" asked Lt. Jenkins.

"I am," Lauren heard herself say, the words sounding as if they were being spoken by another person.

"Ma'am I'm going to give you a number to reach us at here at the station. We've called in reconnaissance planes and our best search and rescue team leader is being deployed as we speak.....Ma'am is there anything else I can do for you? Do you have any other questions...Ma'am?"

"Mom? You don't look good. Are you O.K.?" Evan said as he looked up at her.

Lauren dropped her phone to the tile floor and it broke into several pieces.

# Chapter 10

A loud knock at the door woke Peter who was sleeping on the couch in the living room of his small log cabin. Winnie, his yellow lab and partner of 8 years began to bark viciously at the sound.

"Dammit, shut up Win", he ordered, pulling on a pair of athletic shorts.

He rubbed his eyes and the living room became clearer. There was still an empty glass and a half-filled bottle of Jim Beam on the end table. A newscaster spoke in French from the television that had never been turned off the previous evening. The woodstove had not been stoked and the room was chilly.

Peter approached the door and pulled back

the curtain to see young Officer Marchont standing on his porch. He was a good kid, young and excited about being a Mountie. Well over 6 feet tall, bespectacled and painfully skinny, he stood proudly in full uniform on the porch. Peter could hardly recall when he felt that way.

"Marchont. What the hell brings you way out here?" asked Peter as he opened the door, the cold blast of morning air striking him in the face.

"Good Morning Sgt. McEwan sir. Lt. Jenkins sent me. Seems we have another one sir, a bush plane has gone missing somewhere over the Nahanni."

*Great, here we go again,* Peter thought to himself.

Peter continued to wake from his fog and he found himself staring off at a squirrel playing in the snow under a pine in the side yard.

"Sir?"

"O.K., kid. Tell Jenkins I'll be there in an hour and he should call all the usual pilots we use for sweeps. Try to get a flight plan from the missing plane too. I'll be down in an hour or so."

"Yes sir," chimed Officer Marchont, as he turned for his truck.

"And hey, Marchont," Peter yelled to his fellow Officer.

"Yes sir?"

"Enough of this 'Sir' shit. We're not at the academy, we're not even at the station. We are in the middle of the woods in the Yukon at my cabin. Call me Peter."

"You got it Sir, errr ...I mean Peter."

Marchont still looked nervous as he closed the door and drove off down the muddy road.

Peter laughed to himself. Closing the door he went to the kitchen and filled Winnie's water bowl before heading to the bathroom to rid himself of the previous night's whiskey. He looked in the mirror and was not impressed with the face looking back at him. His hairline was receding at an alarming rate and the wrinkles at the corners of his eyes looked deeper.

*Do most 46-year-old men look this rough,* he wondered as he splashed water on his face.

He certainly felt old. Lately, the life of an RCMP officer was getting to him. For his entire adult life, he had been a loyal servant of the Canadian government. Four years in the Canadian Marines and almost another 25 for the

Royal Mounted Police, the last twelve of which he had been stationed in the Yukon at the Watson Lake detachment.

When he was younger, life on the edge of civilization was all he longed for, excitement and adventure. Well, he'd gotten all he wanted and more.

Sgt. Peter McEwan was regarded as the best search and rescue leader in the Yukon and possibly all of Canada. For more years than he could remember he had been the 'go-to guy' every time a hiker went missing. Or a hunter became stranded in the snow. Or some outdoor enthusiast broke their leg in a rafting excursion and needed an airlift.

Or a plane went missing.

He had an innate sense for it, always able to put himself inside the mind of the missing or injured person. How would they react, which direction did they go? Were they strong-willed or scared? He almost always found them.

More often than not he found them dead.

He was sure this bush pilot was no exception. In his career, he had searched for fourteen downed planes, nine in the Nahanni alone. He had found twelve. They were always 'recovery' missions. Never had he found anyone alive at a crash site. Perhaps that's why he liked looking for outdoorsman and hikers better. At least there was a chance he'd find someone alive.

Peter dressed himself in an unclean uniform from the previous day and went to the kitchen to start the coffee pot. He reached down and scratched Winnie's ears. She wagged her tail and gave him her very serious 'Let's go to work' stare.

Winnie was a yellow Labrador retriever, very small for her breed and more of a butterscotch color. Sickly skinny, with piercing black eyes, she and Peter were inseparable. She was the fourth rescue dog Peter had worked within his career and far and away his favorite. She had a determination he'd seen in no other working dog. She had a nose that could track anything and would work to the point of exhaustion.

When Peter showed up to the RCMP canine training academy in Edmonton eight years earlier they could not push Winnie out the door fast enough. She was a runt and the smallest of all the dogs in her class. Although talented, she seemed to dislike everyone, human or canine.

Constantly fighting or completely ignoring her trainers she was on her way to expulsion. That's when Peter showed up and after one day of working with her he said, "I'll take her."

He loved her feisty nature and determination. He loaded her in his truck and headed north saving her from a life as a pet on some forsaken farm somewhere in Alberta and saving himself from a life of loneliness.

These days found Peter and Winnie tolerating each other most of the time. Both stubborn and antisocial they were a perfect fit, either at work or at home. They were fiercely protective of each other and although neither ever showed it, they had a deep love for each other.

When Winnie was fed they loaded up the truck and headed to the station in Watson Lake.

"C'mon Win'. We've got another corpse to find."

# Chapter 11

Erik didn't know the temperature when he awakened from his half-sleep but it must have been somewhere in the thirties. He could see his breath and he was uncomfortable all night, partially from the cold but mostly from the throbbing pain in his left hand and wrist.

Stumbling from the plane he took one last look around to take it all in. The fog had settled in overnight and he could no longer see the tree line far below that would be his goal. Sparkling frost covered the yellow skin of what was left of the Moose. John passed through his thoughts one last time, he had called out for him several times in the night but there was no response.

It was time to set the plan in motion. The first point of order was to build a sled of some sort to pull the few valuable items he had recovered. There was plenty of sheet metal covering the ground so Erik found some, a square four by four-foot piece. With his good right hand, he bent the edges upward, turning it periodically so all sides would be of equal height. Bending the metal was not easy but Erik oddly found the work enjoyable as it gave him a purpose. Panic had not yet set in and perhaps he was still in a mild form of shock.

When he finished he had what resembled a kind of oversized cake pan. Erik was not sure who had packed the fifty-foot of paracord but he was glad to have it. He had read somewhere that ligature of some kind was one of the most important survival needs in this type of situation. Using his pocket knife and a stone, he punctured holes in his new sled and slid the paracord through to use as a tow rope.

The sun was breaking over the top of the mountain to the east and Erik welcomed the warmth on his face. He was still in an enormous amount of pain, his chest aching with every deep breath, but a new sense of direction left him focused. It was time to load his supplies. He used one of the green raincoats to wrap his sleeping bag, he figured he would need the warmth at night and a wet sleeping bag would do no good.

A pleasant surprise was finding a pair of rain pants in the same package. He stored them for later. He packed the remaining socks and a sweatshirt in the backpack along with the magazine, the now empty water bottle, and the lone granola bar. The broken tackle box he had found included some line and a few hooks. He put on the remaining raincoat.

Using the remaining paracord he secured the whole load to his makeshift sled. On his right hip, he had his gun with thirteen in the clip and one in the chamber. He hoped to use it only to possibly hunt and not to protect himself as the hunted.

The last thing he did was place Gus's lighter in his front pocket.

Erik pulled the sled to the edge of the ledge and looked at the steep grade below.

"Well shit, here we go," he sighed to himself.

Taking one last look around he couldn't help but let out a little chuckle at the absurdity of the situation he was now in. He decided that the best option was to tie the sled to his waist and let it down slowly in front of him as he started down the grade. This trip would be made largely on his backside. He began to slide down on his rear, the weight of the sled not as much of an obstacle as he had thought it would be.

Using his feet as an anchor on the rocks he would slide a little at a time. One false step and he could be lurching forward and his trip would be over fast. After a few minutes, he had traversed only about fifty yards down the hill. The pain in his hand and ribs was intense. He had to stop to catch his breath and that is when he looked uphill and a glint caught his eye.

From this new vantage point, he could see more of the mountain. What he saw, high above on an unreachable ledge and barely visible, was the rest of the plane.

It was burned beyond belief and much more of a mangled mess than the tail section Erik had survived in. Sitting on a small ridge, which was approximately two hundred feet above the tail, Erik could see that he never could have reached it. His guilt for not continuing the search for John was assuaged partly by the location of the wreckage and partly by the fact he believed no one could have survived what he was looking at.

While sitting there contemplating his situation another surprise appeared, perhaps a miracle of some sort. Not ten feet to his right Erik saw another backpack. He slid across the sharp rocks and grabbed it. It was another of Johns, as it had a tag saying so attached to it. Erik opened the zipper and let out a laugh so hard he winced at the pain in his ribs.

In the bag were more socks, thermal underwear and sitting on top, somehow unbroken, the most beautiful bottle of Canadian Mist Erik had ever seen. How that bottle was still intact was a mystery, but Erik was happy to have it.

"Thanks, Buddy," he said and gave a nod up the mountain. Never a religious man, he was somehow moved and believed John's spirit was with him now.

Erik carefully wrapped the whiskey in tube socks and placed it deep in the backpack. Attaching the second pack to his sled he then continued his trek down the ridge. Moving only a few yards at a time, as his backside was killing him; he was determined to make it down to the tree line. He wasn't sure he could survive a night on this slope with the cold and wind. The rain was holding off but it had become very overcast. Dampness overwhelmed him from the sweat and fog.

Erik knew from his research that sundown was around eight PM and he was intent on making the few thousand feet down before then. His broken left hand barked every time he set it on the rocky terrain to study himself. This is how he continued on all day long, hour after hour.

Lauren and the boys became the thought that kept him going. How worried they must be by now. There had to be some reason he'd made it through the crash. Dying on the side of a mountain would be a disservice to their love. He knew he would press on for them but he also knew what the human body was capable of and he had to be careful not to put himself at risk.

Erik went about his work all day long, slowly lowering the sled before him and then sliding on his rear for a few yards. His body ached and his shin was bleeding again. He knew he was becoming dehydrated but there was no chance of finding water where he was so he had to press on.

Eventually, after several hours and several rest stops, the shapes of the trees became clearer and clearer. Soon he could make out the branches and other small details. It was almost dark when he reached level ground.

High altitude scrub pine covered the area Erik finally dragged his aching ass into. He leaned against the first tree he reached and let out a sigh of relief. Looking back up the hill he was surprised to see that he could still make out the ridge he had traveled from. He figured he had slid down about four to five thousand feet. In his research for the trip, he'd read that the highest peak in the Mackenzie range was eleven thousand feet. This meant he was halfway to the bottom.

Parched from thirst Erik, now on his feet, pulled his sled about a hundred yards into the stand of pine. Using the broken limbs that covered the ground, he built little walls against the base of two trees and covered his little shelter by tying a raincoat atop with paracord. He laid out the sleeping bag and emptied the load of the sled inside. It was the roughest of shelters ever built but if it protected him from any rain or wind at all it would be well worth the work.

It had begun to rain lightly and Erik unpacked his sled, putting the packs inside of his shelter. He then pushed the empty metal sled into an opening hoping to catch some rainwater in it overnight.

With his last bit of energy, he pulled himself into the little fort and wrapped himself in the tattered sleeping bag. He was thirsty and in an enormous amount of pain but he was content. He had made it through his first day and if he made it through one he could make it through another.

Besides, Erik had an ace up his sleeve. His attention to detail and knack for preparation was about to pay off in abundance. See, Erik knew where he was. Calculating the time of the cursed flight, and the starting point, there was only one place he could be.

Erik's fight for his life would be taking place in the toughest of all countries. He was somewhere inside the massive Great Nahanni National Park Reserve.

# Chapter 12

Sleep did not come easy that night. Erik sat with his back against a tall pine, a raincoat for a roof with little protection from the elements. It was lightly raining on and off and a slight wind would blow from time to time. Dampness engulfed Erik's body and the sweat from the day's long climb down off the mountain had left his clothes soaked.

The temperature was no more than forty and Erik started to seriously worry about hypothermia taking over his body. Thankfully he had found a couple of pairs of dry tube socks from the backpack and was using them as gloves. Periodically he would flex his feet and his good hand and try, best he could to keep the blood flowing.

Erik promised himself that if at all possible

this would be his last night without a fire. Deciding to keep his mind busy he began to play memory games. Knowing he was somewhere in the Nahanni, he decided to try and remember all he could about what he had read. Always the preparer and an avid reader he had studied the park extensively even though he knew he probably would do no more than fly over it. John and he had considered touring the park as part of their trip, but time and money constraints led to them deciding against it. Now, here he was, fighting for his life in the great park.

The Great Nahanni National Park reserve was first settled by the native Dene people of Canada as far back as nine thousand years ago. Many years later it was mapped and explored by fur traders in the early eighteenth century. Most of the small towns that existed today started out as small trading posts in those early days. By the mid-nineteenth century, the Klondike gold rush was well underway and legends of the ancient peoples who lived in this area spread like wildfire.

Although several companies explored the area no significant gold was ever found. When Willie and Frank McLeod, two prospectors of the era, were found headless many believed the area was cursed. People believed that the brothers had found a large cache of gold and were killed by some mysterious force to forever hide its location. Several geographical landmarks in the park still bore names referencing the incident. Features such as Headless Ridge, Headless Creek, Funeral Range, and Dead Man Valley can still be found on maps of the park to this day.

Aside from the folklore of the park, Erik knew many facts as well. The park was a remnant of the last great ice age nearly two million years ago, and in fact, the mountains in the park were really just an extension of the American Rockies. The park had recently been expanded by the Canadian government to cover nearly eleven thousand square miles. Although the park was not exactly symmetrical in shape, it was about 100 miles wide and 100 miles long, with a little piece coming off the northwest corner. Erik thought that on a map it resembled the Big Dipper.

Perhaps the most useful piece of knowledge he had was that the park was split in half horizontally by the Great South Nahanni River. Along this river were four distinct canyons, basically stages if you will, each with its own steep walls, falls and elevation changes. The river itself emptied out of the park at Nahanni Butte joining the Laird River where there were small towns and settlements. Within the park itself, there were no permanent settlements. The Canadian government allowed guided tours and river rides for thrill-seekers and conservationists. But at no time was anyone ever living in the park.

Many different types of wildlife existed inside the park and this was a major concern for Erik. He knew that timber wolf and grizzly bear encounters were a very real threat. Even large moose and caribou could be dangerous to a human. He had exactly 14 rounds in his pistol and those were for hunting and warding off predators. He must be careful, as he was right in the middle of the food chain in this wild country.

Even though dangerous animals were roaming about there were also many harmless creatures that Erik may have to use as a food source. Snowshoe hare, mink, and beaver were aplenty throughout the park. Falcons and different types of hawks roamed the skies. The rivers and streams were filled with trout and perch. Even bison and wolverine could be found inside the park.

Erik knew the terrain would probably be his biggest battle. Although there were some plains and forests, it was largely a rocky and rough terrain. Drastic elevation changes could be expected. In the wet season, moss and lichen covered many of the rocks and boulders and this would cause slippage and poor footing. Erik's injuries were severe enough that he could not afford a fall of any kind.

Then there were the elements. Erik knew that the Nahanni was entering its autumn season. Temperatures would be as high as sixty and as low as twenty after the sun went down. Rain could be expected and it even had been known to snow in the Nahanni in September. Erik could avoid severe winds and rains by hiding along ridges and under ledges and caves but there was nothing he could do about the cold.

So there sat Erik Keller, unable to sleep in the freezing rain and cold, his head full of useless facts. It didn't really matter what he knew of the area. He was badly injured, ill-prepared, had very few supplies and not a soul on Earth knew where he was. It would come down to one thing if he was to survive this ordeal, and that was will. Even then it would take a tremendous amount of luck and good fortune to find his way out of this beautiful prison. Eric thought of his wife and children, the worry and hell they must be going through. Of course, they, and all law enforcement officials, must think he was dead.

A strange light started to fill the stand of pine and Erik knew the sun must be breaking over the mountain. It was time to start what would be a treacherous journey. One he hoped would find him alive and back with his family.

# Chapter 13

Peter slowly motored down the dirt access road that led to town. He liked to take in nature and wildlife in the area and promised himself long ago never to take the Yukon's beauty for granted. It was about 5 miles from his log cabin to the center of town. Peter's government-owned pickup truck was well over ten years old and a beaten mess due to many miles of travel in this hard country.

Winnie rode shotgun with her tan head out the window, her steely eyes on the lookout for danger or possibly even a meandering squirrel.

Peter had been having some serious thoughts about the direction of his job and life recently. His last case had not ended well and had left him jaded and angry. Two young women in their early twenties thought it would be swell to take a break in between semesters at University and hike along the Toobally Lakes region, an area with no existing trails. They had checked in with Officers at the detachment and they were well provisioned with all the appropriate gear and maps. Peter was not on duty when they left if so he would have advised against the trip.

Alas, they went along their way. When they hadn't checked back in after two weeks, as they had promised, the RCMP contacted their families and began a search. Peter and Winnie were once again called into duty.

The father of one of the girls was a member of the Canadian parliament and the search became a national story in the southern cities. A certain amount of pressure was put on the RCMP by politicians to find these girls alive. Careers, funding, and promotions were all under scrutiny if it didn't go well. Peter would normally be in charge of all search and rescue in the greater Watson Lake area, but several high ranking officers were flown in. High tech infrared search planes and all the latest expensive gadgetry was on hand. Much of the advice given by the seasoned Officers of the Watson Lake detachment was ignored. It was bureaucracy at its worst.

In the end, nearly two weeks into the search, it was Peter and Winnie who had found them. Winnie had picked up their scent the day before and Peter had a hunch they had become lost and were heading west trying to get back to Watson Lake.

Their bodies were in terrible condition, scavenging animals had been feeding on them for some time. They had probably become too weak to continue or possibly one was injured and wouldn't leave the other. A tent was lying on its side, torn and weather-beaten. Peter looked for a note or some sign of what had happened but, like it was in many of these cases, nobody would ever really know what had transpired.

Peter radioed in his location and an extraction team retrieved the bodies. Lt. Jenkins, who had been in line for a promotion, was made the scapegoat and basically told to stay in Watson Lake or retire. The whole affair had left Peter with a bad taste in his mouth and a certain degree of anger towards the government he had served all these years.

His sister Judy had been after him for years to retire and move to the northern suburbs of Toronto. Their parents had long ago passed and Judy, her husband, and their two sons lived there. Peter had visited twice a year for several years and enjoyed himself each time.

Maybe, he thought, it was time.

He had severe doubts if he could adjust to civilian life. Most of the past 25 years he had spent up here in the north country, far from the hustle and bustle of modern life. He had become a loner and had only a few short term romantic relationships since he moved up here. The Town of Watson Lake had only 800 people and the entire area he patrolled held maybe a few thousand and many of them were native peoples. Being alone just seemed easier.

Yes, he thought as he pulled into the station, maybe it was time for him and Winnie to try their hand at a whole different game.

As he opened the door he noticed Lieutenant Jenkins working the phones. Ron Jenkins was a short, broad-chested, graying man who didn't take foolishness lightly. He'd been with the RCMP for nearly forty years and was as tough as they came.

He and Peter held great mutual respect for each other.

"About time you showed up, McEwan! " the grizzled Lt. joshed at Peter, a twinkle in his eyes.

"Hey, better late than never. What are we looking at Ron," asked Peter?

"Bush plane down somewhere between here and Deline. A pilot and two passengers on their way to an outfitter to fish Great Bear Lake. I've got two planes in the air and I'm trying to get Larry Deauchamp over in Ft. Simpson to help out."

"Good, that's a good start."

The RCMP had been given an annual stipend by the government to hire local bush planes for aerial searches for downed planes and lost hikers. A lot of this funding had dried up lately, due to the failure to find the girls alive, or at least that was the opinion of the Officers in Watson Lake.

"With our funding, we will be lucky to get three days out of those planes Lt.," Peter stated. " Do we have a starting point? Anything based on the last radio transmissions?"

"That's why you're here. We need you to talk to the airport managers in both Deline and here to see what times they left and were expected to arrive. All we know is Deline called us and said they never landed last night."

"O.K. I'll head over there and see what I can find out."

The Watson Lake RCMP detachment consisted of only eight officers and usually, only four of them were on duty at any given time. Before Peter left he gave young Officer Marchont an order to round up all the guys.

It would be all hands on deck for the next couple of days.

# Chapter 14

The last 24 hours had been the most difficult of Lauren's life. After her phone call with the Officer from Watson Lake, everything had become a blur. She, of course, made several more phone calls. She had contacted several Canadian law enforcement agencies, the hunting guide in Deline, Watson Lake to speak with Lt. Jenkins again and of course Erik's parents. Everyone said the same thing, let the Royal Canadian Mounted Police handle things and wait by the phone.

She had called Calvin back from school and when he arrived she had to have the conversation she had been dreading. Both boys sat at their family dining room table while a heartbroken Lauren calmly explained that Dad's plane hadn't arrived in its last destination. It may simply be a mistake but Canadian authorities would be conducting a search. There was no need to get worked up and there was nothing they could do but wait for more information. Were there any questions?

"Mom, do they think his plane crashed," young Evan softly asked.

"I don't know, Honey. It's possible," Lauren could feel the tears welling up her eyes as she did her best to remain calm for her boys.

It was silent at the table for a bit before Evan again broke the silence.

"I'm not worried, Mom. You shouldn't be either, Dad is pretty darn tough and he will come back to us, I'm sure of it."

With this, he pushed back his chair and wrapped his arms around his mother's neck. The flood gates opened as Lauren felt her youngest son's love and she cried openly, squeezing him tight.

From across the table, she could see Calvin's face. A look of dread filled his eyes. He was nearly a grown man and unlike eight-year-old Evan, not naive. Lauren could tell that Calvin thought his father was dead already. At that moment, whether it was emotionally healthy or not, she decided that she would not let anyone give up hope.

"Calvin. Calvin, look at me. We are going to get through this. We don't know a damn thing yet. Your father would never give up on us and we're not going to give up on him. Do you understand me?"

A lone tear rolled down his cheek, "Yes, Mom. I understand. But what do we do now?"

"I need you boys to hold the fort down here and be men for me. I'm going to Canada to make sure everything's being done to find Dad."

So, several hours later there she was on a midnight flight to Juneau. She wasn't sure if it was the right decision to leave her boys in the wake of a potential tragedy. All she knew was she had to get up there and do something, to get some kind of an answer.

She had called Erik's mother to come to stay with the boys, and she had a long talk with Calvin about being sensitive to Evan's age and to be careful about what he was saying. Erik's father and brother had taken point on informing family members and continued to work the phones trying to get any help or information on the search.

Sitting in the back of the plane Lauren didn't know exactly what she would do when she arrived at Watson Lake, only that she must get there. Erik was the love of her life and she wouldn't just sit idly by and be a helpless widow.

Tears came and went as she silently sobbed throughout the flight. Her spirits were lifted slightly, surprisingly, halfway through the flight. An older woman, perhaps sixty and wearing a red scarf on her head, took Lauren's hand in her own. She said nothing at all; she might not have even known English for all Lauren knew. She just held her hand and smiled.

"Thank you," Lauren said through her tears.

They remained that way, hands clasped tightly, for the remainder of the flight.

# Chapter 15

The sun was up and with it so was Erik, his determination and spirits surprisingly high. He was tired but buoyed by a general knowledge of what lies before him. It had been a long cold night but it was warming now.

He approached the homemade sled he'd left in the clearing and saw that it held maybe an inch of water. Erik fell to his knees and greedily sucked at the puddle until it was gone. It was probably only two or three ounces of water but it was refreshing and he knew he had to stay hydrated.

The day before he had descended about 5,000 feet to the pine stand he had spent the night in and he figured he had at least that far left to go before he reached the bottom of a valley or river bed. Erik knew he had to go south. What he didn't know was whether he had crashed above or below the South Nahanni River.

He decided that it didn't matter. If he was north of it, a southern route would lead to the majestic river and he would gladly follow it to civilization. If his crash site was south of the river he knew that by walking south he would eventually leave the park and he would run into Yukon Highway 4 that led directly into Watson Lake. Either way, by Erik's reckoning it would be nearly a one hundred mile trip through unforgiving terrain.

As eager as Erik was to head off, he knew that he must take care of his body. He stripped naked and sat on the sled. It was time to clean and redress his wounds.

"Sorry, John", he said aloud as he twisted the cap off the bottle of whiskey.

Tempted as he was to take a slash of the brownish alcohol, he knew it would be best used for cleaning his cuts. Pouring some across a tube sock he first treated his head wound. The whiskey stung as he scrubbed the cut on his hairline. When he was finished he retied the sock 'bandana' around his head. Next was the cut on his right shin. Erik removed the socks he had tied around the wound and was shocked to see fresh blood seep from the deep laceration. He poured a small amount of whiskey directly into the gash. Immense pain roared through the area and Erik found himself gritting his teeth together to keep from screaming.

Infection was a real worry and he knew what he was doing was necessary. When his wounds were cleaned and wrapped Erik put on dry socks, a pair of John's brightly colored underwear and redressed in his torn jeans, tee-shirt and a flannel shirt. This was all accomplished very slowly due to the pain and swelling in his left hand. It was unbelievably large and discolored and pain screamed through his body every time he bumped it. It was especially difficult trying to tie his boots.

He must find some way to wrap or cast his hand, he decided. Going through his backpack of limited supplies he found the answer. First, he placed a couple of socks over the hand. They were the same ones he'd used as gloves the previous night. He took the magazine he had found at the crash site and tore out a handful of pages. He placed these pages into his pack for use as possible fire starter later on. Taking the remainder of the magazine, he coiled it around his left wrist and hand.

Finally, he grabbed the duct tape he had found. He hoped there was enough left on the roll as he pulled it around the magazine and bound his hand. He was happy that he was able to go around the entire magazine five times before the roll of tape was empty.

Sitting back on the sled Erik felt a little sense of pride as he admired his improvised cast.

"Damn, that's not half bad," he exclaimed to nobody.

Putting the cap back on the whiskey he carefully wrapped it in the remaining underclothes and put it back in the backpack. Erik coiled up the tattered, damp sleeping bag and tied it up with paracord. He packed all the rain gear in the other pack and tied everything together on the sled.

The last thing he did before leaving was to eat his lone granola bar. This scared him as it was the only food he had and he didn't know when he would eat again. Some of his rear teeth were still slightly loose and he was slow and careful as he took his first bite. There were only four or five bites in the whole thing but Erik thought it was delicious and could actually feel a slight fullness in his empty stomach. He realized at that moment that he hadn't eaten in nearly three days.

Taking one last look around, Erik took a deep breath and headed off into the pine stand. He wasn't really sure what direction to head, only that he must go downhill. Heading west through the little patch of the forest he saw his first sign of wildlife. A single squirrel saw him approaching and scurried up a tall pine. Erik felt encouraged by the sight and was left feeling a little hopeful. At least he was not the only one up there.

After about thirty minutes of pulling the sled through relatively flat terrain, he exited the little forest. Erik found himself standing on another ridge and far below he could see a wooded valley. It was perhaps another couple of thousand feet down but reachable and not nearly as steep as the mountainside he had slid down the previous day. Beyond the valley, Erik saw more peaks and ridges, but this didn't concern him as he only wanted the get as low as possible and search for running water.

Much like before Erik slid slowly on his rear, lowering the sled down before him. He made a much faster time because the grade was easier and was even able to walk upright a good part of the time. By midday, he was at the bottom and the patch of forest lay before him.

To Erik, these woods looked greener and healthier than the stand he had spent the previous night in. He figured it was due to the lower elevation. Spruce and fir had now joined the pine and the forest seemed livelier as he headed off into it.

Several times he stopped, as when he went to fast his breathing sped up, causing pain in his damaged ribs. He was able to keep the pain out of his mind as he pressed on. Above the trees he saw his first bird, a falcon, as it scanned the floor of the forest for potential meals. He marveled at its grace as it soared above the treetops.

Erik knew he was in between two peaks as he walked along the wooded valley and it was thick enough that he could not make out any of the features on the inclines of either side. Slightly disheartened that he had found no streams or tributaries yet, Erik pressed on. After a while, he came out of the forest and in front of him was another ridge.

He had prepared himself for this. Not every part of this trip could be downhill, there would be times that he would have to climb up and over rocky hills and terrain. This would be the same even if he found the Nahanni River. It wouldn't be like walking along the Mississippi river, flat on both sides, all of these waterways were cut though solid rock over the course of several thousand years.

Tired, and faced with this new obstacle, Erik decided it was best to make camp. He was in danger of becoming severely dehydrated and he was trying to be mindful to rest his damaged weary body. Retreating back a few hundred yards into the woods Erik started to prepare for the night. It was starting to get cooler and now that his body had stopped moving the cold was much more noticeable.

The good thing about this particular patch of forest was that the floor was covered with broken branches and old, blown down growth. Erik placed a thick, ten foot long, branch over the edge of two large boulders. He then began to collect shorter branches or small logs to cover the back. He was building a lean-to, just the way John and he did when they were kids. They would sleep under these homemade shelters after a day spent fishing and pretend they were in the deep wilderness instead of the woods behind their childhood homes.

There was no pretending now as Erik busied himself with his work and before long he stood in front of a decent little shelter. Now it was time to keep a promise to he had made to himself and prepare a fire. He did not intend on spending another night shaking and freezing. Placing small rocks in a circle in front of his lean-to he made a fire pit. Gathering several branches and twigs of varying sizes he built himself a nice cache of fuel for his fire.

He grabbed a page of the magazine from the first backpack and ripped it into small pieces. Next, he made a small teepee of dried twigs over the papers the center of his fire pit. Reaching into his front pocket he pulled out Gus's lighter and bent down. The first flick of his thumb on the lighter produced a beautiful blue flame and Erik held it against the paper until it ignited.

The little twigs instantly began to take flame as he lightly blew air underneath them. Within minutes a healthy fire was roaring and Erik basked in its warmth as he fed it. He was feeling very happy at that moment, so much so that he almost forgot how hungry and thirsty he was.

Erik pulled the little sled and all his supplies under the lean-to, it didn't look like rain but he was determined to keep everything dry. Uncoiling the sleeping bag he pulled his tired beaten body deep inside. It was dark now, only the light of the orange crackling fire was visible. Erik did not even hear any sounds in the forest. He lay in his bag, his head very close to the fire and fed sticks and branches into it until it grew.

His last thoughts were of his sons before his tired body surrendered and, for the first time in days, he fell into a real sleep.

# Chapter 16

Erik was awakened by a noise he did not recognize. He opened his eyes and lay very still. The fire had burned out and he was chilly, but he remained quiet and didn't move for several minutes. Just as he was passing it off as nothing more than his imagination, he heard it again.

It sounded like the shuffling of feet on the forest floor, not the sound a squirrel would make, but something bigger. Slowly, and in a great deal of pain, Erik slid out of his sleeping bag and crawled out of the lean-to. His body had stiffened up considerably overnight and every movement put him in agony. The sun was almost up and the forest was coming alive, the shadows of the trees were taking shape.

He reached down and pulled his pistol from its holster if this noise was coming from a bear he wanted to be prepared. Creeping along in the direction of the sound he thought, for the first time, that maybe he could kill and eat whatever it was.

As he rounded a group of boulders Erik saw it, a large caribou. Steam rose from the beast's nostrils and its coat was dark and shiny. Its antlers stood tall and Erik panicked a bit when he saw it. The animal had spotted him and they stood there silently for a moment sizing one another up.

The maximum distance you can accurately shoot a handgun is about 25-30 yards, Erik knew this. Alas, the beast was probably closer to fifty yards away. Knowing he may not get another chance he slowly raised his sidearm, let out a slow breath, and fired.

CRACK !!!

The noise of the shot echoed through the trees. The caribou hunched its shoulders and sprang from the site. Erik quickly covered the fifty yards and searched for blood or hair. There was none. He had missed it.

"Goddamit," he yelled out loud.

Erik stood there silently replaying the incident

in his head and after a few minutes, he holstered his weapon and slowly limped back to camp. Maybe he should have been more patient, this had been a golden opportunity and he'd blown it.

Erik went through what would become his routine. Cleaning his wounds with whiskey, changing his socks, redressing his forehead, he prepared for that day's journey. His homemade cast was holding up well and the pain in his crushed left hand had subsided a little. He packed the sleeping bag and two backpacks, secured them to the sled and headed off. It saddened him to leave his little lean-to; it had been the most comfort he'd known since the crash.

Moments later he was out of the forest and standing in front of the ridge, the same obstacle that had stopped him the day before. There was no avoiding it this day and Erik knew he could not go another day without water. He was severely dehydrated already, he could feel it in his back and muscles, and he needed to find water today.

Unlike before, when he was sliding downhill, Erik was now pulling the sled upwards. Immediately he knew that it was going to take much more effort. He slowly plodded along one foot in front of the other, trying his best to avoid uneven footing.

Taking breaks every fifteen minutes or so he reached the top of the ridge by midmorning. The view was not unlike what he had seen the entire journey. Rocky ridges, mountainsides, patches of forest. Once he maneuvered back down this ridge there was another valley, another stand of pine.

It was becoming hard not to become discouraged but he knew he had to press on. As long as he was going downhill he would eventually find water, he continued to tell himself. The newest problem he was dealing with was a splitting headache and blurred vision. It had only been four days since he'd had at least a mild concussion but the reality was his body was starting to shut down due to lack of water.

Two hours later he was at the base of the ridge standing before another patch of evergreen. He slowly walked through the new stand of forest, ever vigilant, knowing now that there was wildlife around. He didn't want to miss a chance at another shot at an animal.

He sat on a downed tree and rest for over an hour. Listening to the sounds of the wilderness relaxed him and distracted him from his discomfort. Plus he needed the sun to start setting so he could keep his bearing south.

When he was satisfied that he was going in the right direction he headed off again. The terrain was still rocky and uneven in the forest, but not nearly as bad as the barren ridges he had been forced to navigate. Years of fallen trees and evergreen needles had coated parts of the ground with a nice soft floor.

These woods were a great deal bigger than the other stands of pine and spruce he had been in over the last few days. Erik walked for another three hours and the only ridges and peaks he could make out through the dense forest were far off. Anyway, it was getting dark again and Erik began to fear he may not be able to go on the next day without water. What choice did he have, it was getting dark and he'd have to make camp soon. He could drink the whiskey, it did have a caloric value, but it would just exacerbate his dehydration.

Erik followed the same routine as the previous evening, finding two large boulders, laying a beam across, and covering the back with branches.

He then gathered stones for his fire pit. Pulling his sled inside he headed off to gather firewood. There were less downed limbs on the forest floor here than the previous day. This caused Erik to wander farther than he had before. He was scared to let camp too far out of his sight as his blurred vision and loss of daylight may cause him to get lost.

Erik became frozen in his tracks for a moment. He heard a far off hissing noise.

*What the hell is that?*

Still, in fear of losing his camp, he pressed on ahead. Soon he came to a thick patch of scrub pine, the noise was just on the other side. He became entangled as he tried to push through the bushes, almost lacking the strength to break free. When he reached the other side he saw what was causing the noise.

There, ten feet in front of him was the most beautiful, stony, babbling brook he had ever laid eyes upon.

Erik sprang forward and lying on his stomach, slammed his face into the cold mountain water. It was clean and cold and Erik thought it was the greatest thing he had ever tasted. The water filled his stomach and immediately filled his body with energy. Splashing water on his face, cleaning away the dirt and dried blood, he felt like a new man.

This little stream was no more than five feet across and maybe a foot deep, but it ran clean and strong. Erik stayed at its edge drinking and washing his body for a full fifteen minutes. He made his way back to the camp, grabbed the empty water bottle and returned to the stream to fill it.

Erik knew this was a game-changer, water meant life. It also meant he had a trail to follow. This little flow would take him to a bigger one and yet a bigger one until he reached civilization again. Erik started his fire, slid into his bag and felt a sense of victory. He sipped on his bottle of water until very late into the night. Feeding his fire he knew what the next step would be.

He had to find food.

# Chapter 17

After what seemed like the longest layover of her life, Lauren had managed to get a small plane to Whitehorse. From there a bush plane pilot, who was surprised to have a lone female passenger, agreed to fly her into Watson Lake. She had been traveling for 36 straight hours.

When the pilot taxied up to the hangar at the small airport Lauren's feet were on the ground almost before the plane stopped. She grabbed her one bag and beelined for the manager's office, rapping hard upon the glass window of the door.

"I need to get to the RCMP station right now," she demanded of the poor guy.

When he realized who he was speaking with he grabbed his own truck, flipped the sign in the window to 'Closed', and drove her there himself.

She marched up the steps of the Watson Lake Royal Canadian Mounted Police detachment and opened the door.

"Can I help you?" said a tall, youngish looking man in uniform, who appeared to be no more than twenty-five.

"Yes, I'm Lauren Keller and I'm here to help in the search for my husband Erik. Now, please direct me to the man in charge. Right now, please."

Young officer Marchont stood silently for a moment, the color leaving his face.

"I said NOW!" a tired and obviously determined Lauren yelled.

At this Officer Marchont sprang up, spilling his coffee across his desk, and split for Lt. Jenkins office. He hadn't reached the door yet when Lt. Jenkins came out on his own.

"What in the hell is the racket out here!!"

In front of him was an attractive, blonde woman of maybe forty years in age. She was red in the face and looked as though she hadn't slept in days.

"I'm Lauren Keller, are you in charge?"

"I am the commanding officer of this.......wait.

Did you say Keller?"

"Yes, the wife of Erik."

"Oh my, Mrs. Keller please come into my office. Marchont!! Get this woman a cup of coffee now!"

"Yessir," young Marchont said as he flew to the kitchenette.

Once inside the Office, Lauren found herself sitting in Lt. Jenkins's leather chair in front of a sizzling woodstove. The station was quaint, older with a lot of wood paneling and walls full of maps and photographs of officers. It smelled of men and wood smoke.

"Lt. Jenkins I want..."

"Please. Call me Ron," the grizzled veteran interrupted.

"Ron. I've come along way and I want to know exactly what's being done to find my husband."

"Ma'am, I understand. It's just that we don't usually get family members showing up on our doorsteps when someone goes missing. This is a pretty remote country, I'm shocked you made it here as fast as you did."

"Well, I'm here now and want answers,"

Lauren was getting impatient.

"Of course, of course, you do. Ma'am, we've got three planes searching different grids of the area we think your husband's plane might have gone down. We have a man interviewing both airport managers to find out departure times and expected arrival times. Once we have that information it will allow us to minimize our search area. Four more of my men are prepping to enter the area once we spot any wreckage. This is our standard operating procedure, I'm afraid we have had to deal with this thing far too often up here."

"Is this all of the men at your disposal?"

"It is at this time, Ma'am. We have put in a request for more money for local planes to search on our behalf. There is also talk of an elite search and rescue team from Edmonton possibly arriving tomorrow. The Canadian government is trying to free them up to help us."

"What can I do to help," Lauren demanded?

"Ma'am, with all due respect... nothing. I understand that this is difficult and it's hard to be patient but you have to let us do our work. Ma'am.... where are you staying?"

This question hadn't even occurred to Lauren. She wasn't thinking about anything beyond finding this office and getting some answers. She was exhausted and had single-mindedly been traveling for hours with little advance preparation. But, it was not like there was a Holiday Inn in this tiny town.

"I don't know. I hadn't......"

"Stop right there", Lt. Jenkins knew he couldn't turn this woman away. "We have a bunkhouse in the back. The guys use it in between double shifts. There are two sets of bunks, a shower and a warm stove. You can stay here for the time being. Please, go get cleaned up. Catch a few hours of sleep and when you are up to it, we will go over some maps and get you up to speed."

"O.K. Thank you, Ron."

"Of course."

She stood, took a few steps and turned towards Jenkins.

"Lieutenant......I know that me being here is unusual, I just need to know that you are doing everything you can. I have two young sons that I left at home to be here."

She looked, for the first time since she entered

the station, scared.

"We are, Ma'am. I promise."

With that, she entered the bunk room with her bag.

What was Jenkins to do? Having a civilian stay in the station, especially a female, was against all RCMP regulations. But hell, this woman just came four thousand miles in search of a likely dead husband. The least they could do was make her comfortable and let her feel like she was part of the process. Ron had never in all of his years had a wife of a missing tourist show up at the station. A local, well maybe a couple of times, but usually they were just shipping a body back to wherever the poor dead soul had come from.

"Marchont!!!" Jenkins yelled, snapping from his thoughts.

"Yessir ??"

"Get your ass down to Anita's Diner and grab a special and some pie. We're not gonna let this poor woman go hungry!"

A poor woman indeed, Jenkins thought to himself, she is waiting on a body.

# Chapter 18

Peter McEwan was interviewing the hangar manager in Watson Lake when he got his first decent piece of information. Erik and John's plane had departed for Deline at approximately eight PM the night it went missing. The airport in Deline retrieved a portion of a 'Mayday' call right before 9 pm. Depending on speed this would place the crash site somewhere southwest of the small village of Wrigley, well past the Nahanni and much flatter, easier ground for the search planes to fly over.

Peter relayed this information to Lt. Jenkins at the station so he could narrow down the search quadrants for the hired planes. At Peter's insistence, an RCMP officer from the Watson Lake station was riding as a passenger with each of the three planes. They were all armed with high powered binoculars and McEwan figured two sets of eyes were better than one.

Instead of heading back to the station with Winnie where he would be stuck in the office waiting for new information, Peter had another idea. He would drive to Whitehorse and interview some of the local pilots at the hangar. Nobody in the Watson Lake hangar was very familiar with this Gus Atkins guy and maybe if he knew more about him and his plane he could narrow the search.

The trip to Whitehorse was three and a half hours one way in Peters beat up RCMP issued pick-up truck. That was O.K., more time for him to think and for Winnie to let her long ears blow in the wind. Peter grabbed a bagged lunch from Anita's and headed down Alaskan Highway One.

Along the way he let his mind wander back, through all the searches and all the rescues he had made. When he was young, the few successful rescues he was a part of had made the job worth it. As he had grown older and realized that those happy endings were far and few between, he had become bitter. Maybe he was just old and tired.

Maybe a new adventure was needed. Maybe Judy was right.

He was lonely and as great a dog as Winnie was, he needed companionship. He needed to learn how to be social again. He wanted to travel, trace his Scottish roots, something he'd promised his dying father he would do before he himself ran out of time.

First things first, he needed to have one more happy ending. Even if it was just finding a lost boy scout who wandered off on a day trip. Winnie and he had to go out on a good note, on their own terms. They needed just one more little victory. It probably wouldn't happen on this assignment; a downed plane in the Canadian wilderness seldom had a good outcome.

After a little more than three hours and a few bathroom breaks for Winnie and Peter, they were pulling into the Whitehorse airport. Peter cracked the window and left Winnie in the truck, much to her to dismay. Soon he was sitting in the office of the airport manager.

"Searching for those three up near Deline, Huh?" asked the bald, obese man behind the desk.

"Yeah, afraid so. What do you know about the

pilot, Atkins?"

"Gus? Oh, I don't know, hadn't been flying long. Had a sweet Murphy Moose, though. Yellow and fast. Don't know how a guy like him got his hands on a plane like that."

"What do you mean, 'Guy like that'?"

"Oh, I don't know, he was....ehh...kind of a loudmouth. A braggart. Lotta the guys didn't like him hanging around the hangar. Acted like he knew everything."

"Had he been around here long?"

"No. I've been here forever and he's only been taking passengers up north maybe six months or so. Claimed he'd been flying around Hudson Bay for years."

"Are there any other pilots around today?"

"Yeah, old Chick Hamill is waiting on some folks in the hangar and we've got another arrival any minute."

"Alright, I'm going to head over there, Thanks."

"No problem Officer."

Peter headed out across the tarmac to the hangar as the wind was picking up and blowing cold against his face. He could hear Winnie whining in the truck. When he reached the hangar an older man of about seventy was prepping his plane for a trip.

"Afternoon. Mind if I ask you a couple of questions?" asked Peter.

"Hiya Officer, no Problem. Name's Chick."

Peter squeezed the old man's giant hand and was surprised by his strong grip.

"This guy that went down last week, Gus, did you know him?"

" Ehh, met him a few times. Know-it-all. Always chirping about how he was a big manager in the Tungsten mines back in the day. I didn't believe a word he said."

"Tungsten, eh?"

"Yeah. Nobodies mined there in years. Don't think they even have a runway up there no more."

Just then a little grey bush plane landed on the runway and taxied up to the hangar. The engine soon cut off and a pilot and passenger hopped out and approached the hangar.

"That must be the feller I'm taking up to Great Bear Lake," said Chick.

Peter greeted both the men when they entered the hangar and was asking the other pilot about

Gus when suddenly the passenger chimed in.

"Gus Atkins??? That asshole?  Last time my brother and I hunted up here we used him. He took us damn near an hour out of our way so he could fly over the Tungsten mines and brag about how he worked there."

Peter's interest was piqued.

"How long ago was that?"

"Maybe 6 months ago. We were up here from Billings. We talked to some other outdoorsmen when we got home who had flown with him and they all had the same story. Going outta their way to fly over Tungsten.  And man was that guy full of himself."

Peter had heard enough.

"Thanks guys," and with that, he half sprinted to his truck.

Peter knew, as did the men in the hangar, that the trip to Tungsten was well north of the direct path between Watson Lake and Deline. Peter had to hurry back to the station and redirect the search planes. This new information was a game-changer.

When he hopped back in the truck and opened up the throttle Winnie was happy to have her ears flapping in the wind once again.

# Chapter 19

When Lauren awoke she did not know where she was or what time it was. She lifted her wrist to look at her watch and saw that it was just after five PM local time. Sitting up, she looked around the room and saw the glow in the belly of an old woodstove. It reminded her of her grandparent's stove when she was little.

Realizing where she was, the men's bunkroom in the Watson Lake RCMP station, she was not surprised she had slept so hard and long. The last few days had been a whirlwind and between the tears, stress, and travel, her body must have just shut down. She had enjoyed the use of the shower before she lay on one of the bunks and once her head hit the pillow she was out like a light.

Her mind quickly snapped back to business.

Pulling herself together and opening the door from the bunkroom, she walked down the hallway and into the main station office. Young officer Marchont quickly sat upright at his desk.

"Hello Ma'am. We didn't want to wake you. We got you some dinner from Anita's. That's the local diner. Please, here sit at my desk. I'll warm it up for you. Would you like some coffee??"

"Any word on the search?" Lauren asked directly, ignoring the offer.

"No Ma'am."

"Is there anything I can do to help? I need to be involved in some way. Please."

At that moment Lt. Jenkins entered the room from his adjacent office.

"Mrs. Keller, Please. You need to eat. Anita is the best cook in the Yukon and you need to keep your strength up. After you're done I'll go over some grid maps with you and bring you up to par on what's been going on. Please sit."

Lauren was very hungry; she couldn't even remember the last time she had eaten. Reluctantly she sat down at Marchont's desk. Soon the officer arrived with a warmed plate of chicken and biscuits covered in gravy. She ate quickly and felt her body regaining its strength. This Anita was a damn good cook, and Lauren happily started a piece of apple pie before she finally spoke again.

"Ron," she addressed the older officer," Why isn't the Canadian National Parks Service heading up the search?"

"Great question Ma'am. The National parks have taken huge cuts in funding with the downturn of the economy. Used to be the Parks had their own search and rescue teams. They even had their own planes at one time. I guess the politicians decided it wasn't cost-effective. The parks still have rangers and biologists and such, and they will offer any help they can, but they are very understaffed. In the last decade or so the government has appointed the RCMP as the leaders in all search and rescue operations."

"So, it's just you and your men?" Lauren asked, enjoying a cup of hot coffee.

"We have a discretionary budget for paying local bush pilots for searches, as I explained earlier. That's how we've secured the services of the three planes we have up there now. Other than that it's our local RCMP unit, any other locals we can borrow from, and the park staff. We just recently were given software for satellite imagery. That is Marchont's area of expertise."

"Yes Ma'am, I've been searching areas all around the suspected crash sites all day, and I'll be here all night too," chimed in Marchont.

At that moment all three of them heard someone on the porch of the station and the door opened to reveal Sgt. Peter McEwan, returning from his investigative work. Per usual Winnie was close behind.

"Ron, we got some new info to work with, I want to give the pilots some new grids to search tomorrow," Peter said, not fully in the room yet.

"That's good news. Ehh.... Peter, this is Lauren Keller, wife of one of our missing persons. She flew all the way up here from New York and she is going to be a guest in the bunkhouse for now," replied Lt. Jenkins.

Peter was taken by surprise, as this was not a usual course of events. First off, the beautiful blonde before him had caught him completely off guard and secondly, Ron letting a civilian stay at the station was completely out of character.

"Wow, uhh, O.K." stammered Peter.

"Ma'am this is Sgt. Peter McEwan. He is the

best RCMP search and rescue officer in all of Northern Canada. He is leading up all ground and air operations," Ron informed Lauren.

Lauren Keller took a moment to study this man before her, standing there as he was, speechless. He was tall, broad-shouldered with deep-set eyes. His hair was cut close to the scalp and he was in need of a shave. He looked like a man who had spent the vast majority of his life outside in the weather. There was something very serious and direct about this 'Sgt. Peter'. She liked him instantly; this was a man with the demeanor to find her husband.

"Glad to meet you Sgt. McEwan, now if you've got a moment I have some questions."

"Nice to meet you, Mrs. Keller. I'll try my best to answer any questions you have, but first I need to speak with Lt. Jenkins. Ron, your office?"

With that, Ron and Peter left the room and entered the former's office.

"Really Ron? A probable widow sleeping in the bunkhouse? What are you thinking?" Peter was on the verge of insubordination.

"First of all, calm your ass down Sergeant. This poor woman showed up out of the blue, you know there is not anywhere else here for her to stay. If we don't find the plane and bodies in a couple of days we will kindly send her on her way. You know damn well we don't have the money to keep those planes in the air for more than a few days anyway."

"Fine. O.K. Sorry, I have been on the road all day and I just want to get these maps right. Ron... we've been looking in the wrong spot."

"What? So, what did you find out?"

Peter proceeded to tell Ron of Gus's past passengers, his propensity for deviating from his routes to brag about Tungsten and his unknown and possible sketchy piloting experience. It was decided by the two officers to send all three planes and accompanying RCMP officers into search grids much further southwest of where they had previously been flying.

"Peter, I have some news for you that you probably won't like," Ron spoke quietly, "The government is sending that new group up here, the C.E.R., or whatever the hell they're calling themselves."

"Goddammit, you know they will just get in the way!!!"

Peter was incensed. The C.E.R., or Canadian Elite Rescue team, was a newly formed government group who worked out of Edmonton. The team consisted of ex-military Special Forces officers and was being sold to the public as the best of the best when it came to rescuing operations. The team had recently saved some flooding victims in the northern Toronto suburbs and was enjoying the positive press they had received.

The opinion of all ACTUAL law enforcement agencies was much different. To them, the C.E.R. was largely a publicity stunt, a way of distracting the taxpayers from the fact that many other agencies were dealing with massive budget cuts.

The Canadian government put together this team of 12 'experts' and provided them with flashy uniforms and the newest technology. Hell, they even bought them a top of the line military helicopter to travel in. None of the members had any real experience in the hard, cold, rough territory in the northern parts of the country. They did not know the geography or weather patterns. Most of them had been placed on the team because of some sort of political connection.

It was a plush, fancy job with little real work.

They had earned, in their short existence, a reputation of bullying the local law enforcement agency in charge and then passing themselves off as heroes. This, regardless if they had done any real groundwork or actually rescued anyone. Peter despised them already, but if it meant he could use their tech and manpower he would tolerate them. Besides, Ron and Peter were not ones to easily be pushed around.

Armed with all of this new info, and with a woman now prowling the office, Peter went to work. He poured himself a cup of coffee and, avoiding Lauren, sequestered himself to his office.

# Chapter 20

Morning found Erik rehydrated and somewhat well-rested. His injuries were still very real and painful but his body was still running on adrenaline and instinct. He had actually slept decently and was looking forward to following his new stream, hopefully to bigger waters.

Breaking down camp and cleaning his injuries had become a welcome routine. In the real world, Erik was a clock watcher and had a daily regimen that hardly ever changed. Up at 5 AM, shower and a shave, coffee and fifty-minute drive to prison. He took great pride in never having been late for his entire career.

When the camp was down and packed and the sled filled and secured, Erik headed for the stream. It was only a couple hundred yards away and he was eager to fill his water bottle and drink some more of the cold, crisp mountain water.

He arrived and did just that, heartily downing nearly two full bottles of water. Just as he was putting the bottle away, something downstream caught his eye. Erik could have sworn he saw splashing in the waterway down the stream embankment. Pulling his sled along, he went to investigate. When he reached the area he realized that the little stream was dammed up slightly by a few downed logs, creating a deeper pool of water about the shape and size of an above-ground swimming pool.

Erik sat quietly for a moment staring at the pool. Suddenly it happened again, a splash in the water not fifteen feet in front of him. Fish!!!

Quickly, Erik dug through his pack, remembering that he had a fishing line and a few hooks. He was determined to catch a couple of these fish and possibly have the first solid food, other than a granola bar, that he'd eaten in days. But what would he use for a rod and bait?

Venturing back into the brush Erik found an immature sapling no bigger around than his thumb. He cut it off low to the ground with his knife and cleaned it of all its tiny branches. It was eight feet long and flexible, and after making some tiny notches near the end, he attached ten feet of line and a hook to it.

"This should work just fine," Erik said aloud. It was the first time he'd spoke in a few days and he was surprised by the scratchiness of his voice.

Now he had to find bait, there had to be worms or grubs of some sort in the area. Erik wandered up and down the bank of the stream, turning over rocks and downed logs. Finding the bait should have been the easy part of this, he thought to himself. He was sweating and his head began to ache again, so he sat upon a large rock to catch his breath. It was colder than the previous day, and the sky looked threatening grey. Just as he found himself hoping it wouldn't rain he noticed a little flash between the stones by his feet.

It was a salamander, black with yellow spots. It sat there, right next to his foot for a moment. Taking a deep breath, and tensing himself up, Erik flashed downward quickly with his good right hand. Raising his fist to his face he saw a little tail sticking out between his fingers. He'd caught it!!

Carrying his little prisoner back to the newly discovered fishing hole he worried he would drop his bait.

"Sorry, little guy," Erik exclaimed and he slapped the salamander against a rock, killing it.

Using the pocket knife he cut it into smaller pieces and placed one on the hook. Grabbing the sapling he flipped the line and baited hook into the water as far as the line would go. He worried that with no weight the line would not sink, then he thought maybe it was better off floating atop the water. Erik was considering using a pebble as a sinker when he was shocked by a tug on the line. Pulling hard in one motion with his good hand, he flung the line on to the bank. There at the end of the line, shiny and shimmering, was a fish no bigger than Erik's hand. Overjoyed, he dropped his homemade rod and pounced on the fish, quickly striking it in the head with a stone until it lay still. He sat there for a long time staring at it, thankful and happy. He decided he would catch as many as he could before cooking them, although he was eager to consume it right then and there.

Erik went back to work, baiting the hook and

just as quickly he had caught another fish, this one slightly larger. Similar to the first, they looked like some kind of trout but Erik could not tell the species. John had been the fishing expert of the two. Erik found himself thinking about his friend and how, even in this God awful shitty mess, John would be having the time of his life.

Erik laughed quietly to himself and smiled. When the bait was gone he had three dead silvery fish lying next to his sled. He could have possibly found more bait and caught even more fish but he was eager to eat.

Erik took his sled and fish away from the bank and back into the woods. He gathered kindling and stones and made a small fire pit. Once he had a fire going, and a nice pile of embers, he removed the guts from the first fish. Sliding a stick through its body he carefully balanced it over the coals as if he were a Boy Scout cooking a hot dog. He worried about undercooking the fish and possibly becoming ill, but impatience got the better of him and after a few minutes he found himself removing the fish from the stick.

He placed the cooked fish on a flat stone and used his knife to scrape out the white meat. Erik took some of the meat between his thumb and index finger and placed it in his mouth. It was scalding hot, but once it cooled in his mouth the richness of the meat overwhelmed him.

*When a man hasn't eaten in a week everything must taste delicious.*

He let the meat dissolve in his mouth before swallowing and the feeling of hot food in his belly was strange and satisfying. Before long the fish was gone and Erik set to work cooking the other two. There were only perhaps four or five good forkfuls of meat on each fish, but it was plenty to fill Erik's stomach. When he was done he lay on his back, fat and happy, looking at the sky.

It was still only midday and Erik, now reinvigorated with fish and water, was not going to lose a day of travel. The goal, other than survival, was to reach civilization and eventually, his family.

Erik packed the little sled; this time with his lucky rod attached, he then filled his water bottle and set off. Making his way back to the creek he was going to stick to the plan of following it to a larger river, hopefully, the South Nahanni River.

See, one of the last important things Erik knew

was the details of the big river. He knew that if flowed through four big canyons, running west to east, covering nearly one hundred miles. At the end, the river came upon a few small towns, where hopefully he could find help.

Erik did not know if he would find the river or not, nor did he know how far along it he'd be when he did. What he did know is that he might not have to follow it the whole way to find someone. In Erik's studies of the area, he learned about one of the great, widely unknown, landmarks on Earth.

At the beginning of the fourth canyon was one of the greatest waterfalls ever discovered, Virginia Falls.

Virginia Falls was a huge, breathtaking waterfall. It had a single drop of over three hundred feet, making it twice as high as Niagara Falls. Maybe the most awesome feature was a gigantic spire of rock that split the falls into two at the top. It was called Mason's rock, after the man who had discovered it hundreds of years earlier. Virginia Falls was one of the most visited and photographed sights in the whole of the Canadian wilderness, there was even a helicopter pad nearby.

If Erik could get far enough down the river maybe he could reach the pad. Maybe, just maybe, some tourists would be shocked to see a ragged, bleeding man stumble out if the thick woods.

# Chapter 21

It was very late at night and Winnie was curled up in front of the red-bellied woodstove in Peter's office. The Sgt. had been in there redrawing search grids to assign to the officers and bush pilots in the morning. He had also been avoiding Mrs. Keller.

*She must be asleep in the bunkhouse by now.*

The station was sure to be empty, other than the midnight officer who manned the phones in the back communications room. Peter snuck out into the main office to refill the coffee maker when he was caught.

"Avoiding me, Sgt. McEwan?" a soft voice spoke from a dark corner of the room.

Peter spun to see Lauren, wrapped in a blanket with her blonde hair pulled back in a ponytail, sitting on a couch.

"Avoiding you? Ehh, no Ma'am. Just caught up in my work is all," stammered a nervous Peter.

"Before you disappeared you promised to go over search grids with me. Officer Marchont spent over three hours going over satellite images with me. He would have stayed longer, poor kid, he's so sweet. I insisted that he and Ron go home. Everybody has been so nice. So, now I've been out here waiting for you. The guy that every last officer here insists is the best, 'part bloodhound' as Ron put it. So I'll ask again, why are you avoiding me?"

Peter let out a long sigh. He went across the room, cracked open the door to the wood stove and added a few pieces of maple to the already glowing fire. Rubbing his eyes with his large calloused hands he turned and slowly approached the couch.

"Move over, Ma'am," he said, sounding beaten.

Lauren moved over and a tired Peter sat beside her on the small, brown leather couch.

"Listen, Ma'am. I'm not trying to avoid you. But dealing with families is not my strong suit. We usually have public relations officers for that kind of thing. I'm very good at what I do, but I'm a ground guy. I go into the woods and sky. I search and sometimes I find. What I am not good at is being the bearer of bad news, holding hands and such. And Ma'am, I'm sorry to tell you that more often than not the news is usually bad."

Lauren sat quietly for a moment, staring at this man. There was a great sadness about him, darkness almost like he'd seen more than his share of grief. He came across as lonely and beaten down. She thought to herself what a hard and lonely life it must be in this strange, isolated place.

"First of all, enough of this Ma'am stuff," Lauren spoke, breaking the silence. "It's very sweet and all of you men are so polite, but please call me Lauren."

She continued on, the light from the adjoining office illuminating only one side of her face.

"I'm not naive, Sir. I know how bad this is. I know the likely outcome. I will probably be bringing my husband's body home with me, and maybe not even that. Marchont was able to radio over to Whitehorse earlier and I was able to speak with my two sons. They do not know the seriousness of the situation up here. I'm doing my best to keep it together, and I don't know if leaving my boys was the right thing to do. I am holding on by a thread but I am determined to see this thing through. Do you understand?"

Peter slid back on the couch ever so slightly, a little of the tension leaving his body. This was a strong woman, the kind that kept a man on point. The kind he had never known in all of his years up here alone. He instantly felt a need to connect and not disappoint her and he was confused as to why.

"O.K., if I'm calling you Lauren, you have to call me Peter. Fair enough?"

She smiled warmly, "Fair enough, Peter."

He continued, "How old are your boys?"

"Nineteen and eight. Both are sweet and strong like their father."

As Peter eyed the glowing woodstove his thoughts took him back. Very far back.

"Nineteen is a tough age, not quite a kid, not quite a man. When I was nineteen I was already in the Marines in the Canadian fourth division. I was stationed north of Toronto. My father had emigrated to Toronto when he was a child, came across from Scotland. Inverness, actually. He was all about service to his new country, he was so proud of me. They called me home not six months into my service. They had discovered cancer in his lung; the old man was always a smoker. He didn't last three weeks. He made me promise to go see Scotland someday," He paused a moment. "......I never did get there..."

Lauren could tell that even while sharing this information that Peter was reopening an old wound.

"Scotland. How funny. Erik's family is from there and I was going to surprise him with a trip there this spring," she continued, her voice growing quieter, "I was worried about money and the time away from the boys...... It all seems so silly now."

"Tell me about your husband."

"He is my other half, the love of a lifetime. We went on a blind date twenty years ago and instantly connected. Calvin came along, and before we knew it we were a family. We weren't ready and there were struggles but it only made us stronger. He works as a Corrections Officer back in New York, a job he is not exactly crazy about. But he goes every day, and he has supported me all the way through my doctorate. He never misses any of the boy's games or events. He is as loyal as it gets. This trip was a lifelong dream of his and now I feel like maybe I didn't encourage it enough like maybe I should have been more supportive. He is the glue that binds us all together, he is our rock."

Peter marveled at her devotion.

"Doctorate?"

"Yes, I have a Ph.D. in Business Management. I work for Syracuse University," replied Lauren.

Beautiful, determined and smart. Peter had never even met Erik Keller and was already jealous of him.

"What can you tell me about Erik? Any details that might help me do my job."

Lauren contemplated this question for a moment.

"He is a curious man, he wants to know everything. Our thirst for knowledge is one of the factors that kept us close all these years. He is always prepared. When he takes up a hobby or new interest he is all in. This trip, for example, he was so excited that he'd stay up late reading about the area, or studying maps. We could never even go on a family vacation without an itinerary."

"Go on," Peter encouraged her.

"I don't know. He is just a driven person. ...... I know there is not a good chance he is alive, but if he survived the crash I know he would do everything in his power to get back to us.... I know it."

With this, her strength left her and she began to weep softly.

"I'm sorry."

"No, don't be. This must be difficult, harder than I can even understand," said Peter.

Her eyes were a deep brown and trusting. He felt a comfort with her he hadn't experienced with anyone in a very long time.

"I've been alone up here, married to my job for twenty-five years now. I have never had a wife, I have no children. After my father's death, my mother passed the very next year. When I was done with my service I took this job and ran away up here. I left a lot of cards on the table. I'll never know what it's like to have that strong family connection."

"You have no family left at all?" Lauren inquired.

"I have a sister in Toronto and two nephews. I see them a couple of times a year. She's been all over me to move back down and rejoin the 'Land of the Living', as she calls it."

At this, they both laughed.

"Lauren, I'm sorry for what you are going through now and I will do everything I can to help."

He was careful not to make any promises. She was winning him over but he didn't want to give her the false impression that he believed there would be a happy outcome. Winnie had entered the room and to Peter's surprise, jumped up in Lauren's lap and lay down. Lauren stroked her ears and Winnie let out the sigh of a happy dog.

Peter laughed aloud," This is my mistress, Winnie. She keeps me on my toes."

"How old is she?"

"Eight, but I can see her living to about 25," he laughed, "she's too mean to die."

"Oh, nonsense. She is a big baby," Lauren said, rubbing Winnie's bald belly.

"Come with me, I want to show you something," Peter said, leading her into his office.

Slowly and patiently he showed Lauren the

grid maps. He explained everything in great detail, discussing everything from wind shear to the local topography. He told her about the quickly changing weather patterns and the difficulty of spotting wreckage through the treetops. Lastly, he told her about his discovery of Gus's 'short cuts' and how he believed they were looking in the wrong spot.

"So we have new hope," Lauren beamed.

"Well, a new starting point at least. I think the plane went down in the Nahanni Park, and if we can find it, I can get a crew in there. I'm very familiar with the area."

Peter set himself to rolling his maps back up.

"Thank you, Peter. See, that wasn't so hard," Lauren said, earnestly.

"It's my pleasure Ma'am.....errr, Lauren."

She laughed at this.

"Please, get some sleep," he said, "I've got to get Winnie home. We will be back before eight AM. My officers and pilots have a briefing before they take to the skies. I'll see you in the morning. Goodnight."

"Goodnight, Sgt. McEwan."

Both were left feeling more content and

confident, and both instantly felt a special connection to one another.

Peter closed the door behind him and headed off into the cold night.

# Chapter 22

Erik's adventures in fishing had set him back considerably on his day's journey. It was now midday and, although he was happy to have food in his stomach, he had not covered very much ground. The bank along the stream had been mostly clear to this point, but now Erik was finding himself fighting through thicker brush and this was slowing him down.

To make matters worse the sky was darkening and the wind was picking up. The temperature had dropped to the point Erik was chilly even when moving along. Cold, wind and rain could still very well be his biggest challenge to survival. He hoped to stay dry long enough to make a decent camp before dark.

His physical injuries varied. The cut on his

head no longer bled and the soreness in his cracked ribs had subsided quite a bit. On the other hand, his broken and crushed left hand was causing him a great deal of pain anytime it was bumped or moved incorrectly. The magazine and duct tape cast had held up very well, much to Erik's surprise. His biggest cause for concern was the enormous gash on his right shin.

When he cleaned the wound that morning it was starting to smell and Erik cleaned it thoroughly with the whiskey. The problem was the wound was constantly opening back up and bleeding. Trudging along in the woods did not help Erik with keeping the area clean and he feared a serious infection was imminent.

As he trekked the stream he found he was consumed by thoughts of his family. Were they still holding up hope for him? How long could they be expected to realistically believe he was alive out here? Surely there had been a search, but Erik could still see that ridge and plane in his mind. Above the tree line and below the cloud line, it would be like finding a needle in a haystack.

How would the boys do without him? Lauren

was strong, smart and independent, always had been. But the boys were still so young and impressionable. Could they become the men Erik hoped they would be without a father to guide their way?

Erik found that keeping his mind occupied kept him moving and made him forget his pain, the weight of the sled and the nearly impossible task before him. He was deep in these thoughts when he noticed the sound of the stream had grown much louder. Entering a clearing he was shocked to see another stream, this one slightly larger and coming from the northwest, merging with his little stream.

The two connected in a rocky clearing and made for a much bigger, wider stream. The new flow was almost twenty feet wide and, Erik guessed, about six feet deep. It was moving considerably faster and if it needed crossing, would be a challenge.

All in all, Erik was very happy with his new discovery, it was obviously not the South Nahanni River, but it was flowing strongly south and in the right direction. He was more sure now than ever, that his wreck had to of been north of the great river that split the giant park in two. This meant if he kept heading south he'd have no choice but to run smack into the South Nahanni River.

Bending down next to the water Erik splashed his face. He grabbed his water bottle, filled it and drank. As he was refilling it he noticed a strange marking in the mud of the bank. It was a bear paw print and a large one too.

He feared what he already knew to be true. Now that he was down from the mountains and close to a water source he would be in the direct path of predators. This thought had been with him from the start and one of the reasons he was happy to have a fire each night. Wolves and Grizzlies would be wary of flames. Erik also still had thirteen rounds left in his trusty pistol but they would be needed for hunting as well as scaring off potential threats. His biggest fear was stumbling across a large animal while pushing through the brush, surprising it and being unprepared. Could he draw his gun quick enough with no warning? His odor of blood and sweat must be resonating in the wilderness and he was making a lot of noise busting his way through the woods.

He tried best as he could to stay alert and pressed on.

Erik continued, following the new, larger stream. After an hour or so he noticed the banks steepening on each side of the water. The terrain had become rockier and much rougher. Soon Erik could see that the water ran into a valley with very high ridges, perhaps a couple of hundred feet on each side. He decided it was too early to make camp and he would have to go up and over the ridge.

*Ughh!!,* Erik thought to himself, here we go again with the climbing.

The ridge was steep, not so much as to where he might fall, but enough to make his muscles burn and his heart beat furiously. Using embedded rocks as steps he slowly worked his way up, the cumbersome sled in tow. The higher he rose the more the wind intensified, and it was now burning his cheeks red. Reaching the top of the ridge seemed to take forever and Erik was surprised how quickly the light was fading.

When Erik reached flat ground the wind was howling and he found himself among nothing but boulders. There were no trees or bushes or anything resembling fuel for a fire. He knew he was at the top of the ridge, but it was too dark now to see below. He did not know what awaited him in the morning and Erik now knew he had made a grave mistake. There was little in the way of natural surroundings to keep him out of the wind, and no way to build a fire, and to make matters worse, a light rain was beginning to fall.

Erik knew if he were to survive the night he would need shelter, so he had to work fast. As panic overtook him he searched until he found two large boulders that were close together with only a couple of feet between them. Unloading the sled, now beaten dented and devoid of any paint, he placed it on top of the boulders creating a makeshift roof. It was only three feet high but he was not concerned about headspace, only making a dry, airtight hovel.

Opening both of the raincoats he covered the sled/roof further and placed smaller rocks all around the edges to prevent wind from blowing the whole thing away. He pulled the backpacks and sleeping bag under the roof to keep them dry. He then set himself to piling rocks atop each other to make a rear wall, his hope is that his three-sided shelter would keep him out of the elements.

It was hard work; most of the rocks in the area were round and difficult to stack. Darkness made seeing what he was doing nearly impossible and his injured hand forced him to go much slower than he preferred. Eventually, he had covered most of the open area and created a back wall. Knowing that he had accomplished all he could he crawled inside the little stone fort.

It was a tight fit and when he unrolled the torn and tattered sleeping bag his feet were still outside. He used the backpacks to plug up the few remaining cracks in the back wall. He put on every extra piece of clothing he had. Pulling off his boots, he placed his last pair of extra socks on his feet and crawled into his bag.

The wind was howling now and Erik was very scared his roof would blow off. He pulled his knees tight to his chest and was able to keep his whole body inside the shelter. The large rocks prevented a lot of the wind from getting to him but he still felt its presence. The sound of the rain had stopped so Erik peeked his head out of the open end of the shelter. It was as dark as he had ever seen, and before he drew his head back inside he felt a cold familiar feeling on the end of his nose.

It was a melting snowflake.

Erik truly feared he wouldn't survive the night. The wind, rain and now the snow were his enemy. He could feel the cold right down to his bones and he began to shiver violently. The wind had picked up considerably and it whistled through his stone fort with a high pitch shriek. Maybe this was it.

Minutes turned to hours as he fought to stay warm. He pulled his body into a tight ball and tried to trick his brain by thinking only warm thoughts. His teeth began to chatter and he was more frightened than any other time he could think of since he was a child.

It would prove to be the longest night of Erik's life.

# Chapter 23

Sunlight shone through an opening in Erik's stone tomb. It hit him directly in the face, forcing him to open his eyes. Soft fluffy snow, the type you can blow away like dandelion fuzz, was inches deep in his shelter and surrounded his bag. His hands were numb and the entirety of his body ached, but he was alive.

He didn't move for a moment, instead, he squeezed and wiggled his toes and fingers. Painfully, the blood was flowing in his digits and he was happy for the feeling. Looking to the entrance of the fort he gazed around, making sure it was safe to come out. With great difficulty, he crawled out of his bag, slid his boots on and looked around.

The wind had stopped but it was still very

cold as the sun broke over the hills to the East. Erik turned to the South. What he saw took his breath away and he wondered if he was dreaming or if maybe he had died right there on that ridge.

Below him, clear as a photograph and perhaps still five miles away was a giant roaring river. It was the South Nahanni, he had no doubt. It looked incredible much like every picture he had seen of it. If it had been light when he had reached the top of the ridge that last night he would have seen it then.

He was a couple of hundred feet above it and it was still off in the distance but he had reached his mark. Great confidence came over him and he was more certain than ever that he would find his way out. He had survived the terrible night and now he was being rewarded.

Quickly Erik deconstructed his camp, filling his packs, rolling up his bag and tying it all to his sled. The snow from the previous night was very light and dusty and didn't even cover the entire ground. In fact, it seemed there was more in his rock fort than anywhere else. He was still very cold and decided the only way he could warm-up was to get moving.

Taking a long drink from his half-frozen water bottle he took one last look off into the distance. He was determined to remember this view, far up high and far away from the river. Once he reached its banks he knew that he would not have this angle and the mighty river would become just another landmark. Erik wanted to always see it for what it was to him, a beacon of hope.

He took a deep breath of the cold morning air and started off.

The journey down was, as usual, much easier than it was up. It was less steep and less rocky and within ninety minutes Erik had reached the banks of the stream he had left the night before. Along with the stream came trees and bushes and wildlife. He saw a squirrel scurry up a spruce tree and for a minute considered hunting it. Thinking better of it he pressed on, it would be a waste of a bullet for such a small animal that provided little meat.

He was saddened that he could no longer see the South Nahanni now that he was back to ground level. Alas, he didn't dwell on it much as he knew now, without doubt, that his stream would be leading him to the river soon. He continued to head south along the banks, excitement kept him moving at a brisk pace.

The sun was fully in the sky now and it was mid-morning. Erik gladly felt the warmth on his face and marveled at how, in such a short time, the weather could change so quickly in this country. He was a man renewed as he marched along. Birds chirped in the trees and on more than one occasion he saw a hawk circling, stalking its prey. Other than squirrels he saw no other wildlife.

He took advantage of the stream and drank from his water bottle a few times, but his stomach was screaming. The fish from the day before was a nice morsel but were only slightly filling. Now that the water he was drinking was stretching his stomach out he realized that he was extremely hungry. He would need food and soon.

Erik began to notice as he walked that his stream was picking up speed and the water was becoming rougher. He knew what this meant. He was close now. Rounding a bend in the stream he reached a series of large boulders that had been deposited on the bank thousands of years ago. He scampered atop one of them and there it was in front of him.

The little stream fell about ten feet straight down from a stony ledge in the form of a beautiful waterfall. When the water landed it was now part of the Great South Nahanni River. The stream had joined the river and become one, and oh what a sight!

The river was probably an entire football field wide and the rush of the water and rapids caught Erik off guard. He was astonished at the raw power of the flowing beast and a little intimidated as well. Large sharp and dangerous-looking rocks lined the sides of the river and Erik realized he would have to be extremely careful traversing the edge of it. Even filling his water bottle would be dangerous.

Regardless of the dangers, Erik was thrilled. He now had his guiding light and as long as he stayed along the river, and stayed alive, he knew he'd find civilization. He took in the majesty of the river for only a moment or two and then headed east, in the direction which the river flowed, and started what he hoped would be the last leg of his journey.

By his estimates, and what he had

remembered of his maps, Erik figured he had traveled south approximately fifteen miles. He knew the river ran west to east through four canyons for over one hundred miles. He did not know at what point he had intersected the river. The remaining walk could be anywhere from forty to ninety miles.

It was all guesswork, Erik knew this much, but the constant calculations kept his mind busy and gave him goals to strive for. Making his plan he figured he would walk until late afternoon, set up camp, and hopefully catch some fish for dinner.

Walking along the river was much different than the stream. Where the stream bank was slightly rocky and close to the trees, the river was lined with large vehicle sized boulders and the trees and woods were set back a good distance from the river.

At first, Erik tried keeping to the river, hopping and climbing from boulder to boulder. This proved to be tiring, slow and dangerous. As much as he didn't want to lose sight of the river he decided to retreat to the flatter, safer tree line where he could make better time. He figured as long as he could still hear the roar of the water he was good.

As he traveled he noticed the forest began to come alive. Squirrels were more abundant, birds sang loudly and he even saw the flash of what appeared to be some sort of weasel heading to the river. The trees still consisted of mostly spruce and fir, but the few hardwood trees that were there had begun to shed their colorful leaves. Despite the pain he was in Erik was thoroughly enjoying the scenery.

Hours later, when he noticed the sun starting to reach the tops of trees, he decided to make camp. It had been a great day and he wanted to end it on a good note. Finding some boulders to make shelter had become the easiest part of Erik's day and it took him no time to find some. Before long he had rounded up some downed logs and made a nice little weatherproof lean-to. After building his fire pit from a circle of rocks, he gathered some kindling and firewood. The woods along the river were the healthiest he had encountered yet and fuel for the fire was aplenty.

Erik was excited to fish and possibly eat a good meal before dark. Collecting his sapling rod and a few hooks he headed to the river. In no time he had found some grubs in a rotting log and placed them on his hook. Climbing along the boulder he threw his line into the fast-moving water.

Immediately he knew that catching fish here would not be as easy as the little swell in the stream where he had fished before. The water moved fast and his grub was pulled from its hook almost instantly. Erik found another grub, hooked it better and tried again. The hook and grub would not sink and instead skipped along the top of the river. Maybe this wasn't a bad thing, thought Erik. After all, fly fisherman keep their flies atop the water and the fish strike from below.

Erik let out his line and again his grub was washed away. Again, he found another grub and hooked it. He decided to try to fish the backside of a large boulder where the force of the water wasn't as strong. Finding a much calmer spot he sat and bobbed his grub up and down in the water. For nearly an hour he did this with no luck. Frustrated, and with the light fading fast, Erik decided to head back to camp and build a fire.

He became worried as he left the river. It had been eight or nine days by his count and all he had eaten was a granola bar and three small fish. Hiking the river caused him to exert a lot of his energy, and he was injured and had gone through all of his body fat supply. He needed nourishment badly. He decided that tomorrow he would stay in this spot and hunt for game, even if that only meant squirrels. This terrible ordeal had taken its toll on Erik, both physically and mentally. But at every turn, when he needed a break, he had received one.

This day would be no different.

As a gloomy Erik came upon his camp he heard branches breaking and feet on the ground. He held perfectly still and scanned the dark forest with his eyes. Fifty yards to his left was a large female caribou, with two small yearlings next to her. They had smelled Erik, but they had not seen him yet.

Slowly and deliberately he placed his rod down on the ground. Darkness was now his friend as the animals could not easily see his movements. Erik, for the first time in a long time, pressed the release on his holster and eased his sidearm out. The caribou were facing away from him, the mother's nose in the air, sniffing danger. At any moment they might bolt away, he had to be ready.

Erik raised his gun and placed the day glow sights level with his eyes and the target. He was too far away to be accurate with a handgun and knew he had to close the distance. Keeping the gun raised, he slowly and quietly crept towards the wild beasts. His heart was beating so loudly that he thought his prey might actually hear it and his hands trembled. He had hunted his whole life but never had so much been at stake.

When he had gotten fifteen yards closer and was still undetected, he knew it was time. At first, he placed his sights on the larger caribou, but she was facing away from him. One of the yearlings was standing sideways and made for a better target. Erik took a slow deep breath and let it half out. Aiming as he had been taught as a boy, at center mass, he quickly pulled the trigger twice. Boom! Boom!!

The shots were louder than he had ever remembered hearing before and the sound rang in his ears for a moment. There was a great thrashing about and he could hear the animals escaping through the brush and trees. He didn't see anything at first glance and feared he had missed, but as he approached there it was. Lying dead, shot through the chest with one shot, was the yearling. It had died almost instantly, there was no suffering.

Erik fell to his knees and began to sob.

The outpour of emotion caught him off guard and he cried loudly, tears running down his cheeks. It wasn't necessarily for the young animal, or even for his happiness at the upcoming meal, he was about to eat.

The tears were a culmination of every emotion he had had been burying for the past several days. It was the loss of John, the fear, the hunger, the enormous guilt he felt, the separation from his family, all of these feelings had boiled over and hit him as he stood over the dead animal. He was so very thankful for the moment and so thankful for the opportunity to survive another day.

After a few moments, he gathered himself together and rose from the ground.

Grabbing the young caribou by the back hooves he dragged the animal the few hundred feet to his camp. He remembered leaving his fishing rod and went back for it. Arriving again at the lean-to he stood over the animal. It was a good kill, he decided. The animal probably only weighed eighty pounds, killing the much larger mother would have been a waste.

He untied the paracord pull strap from the sled and slid it through small cuts in the animal's tendons above the rear hooves. After tying the hooves together he tossed the cord over a reachable branch and hoisted the animal off of the ground until it was swinging freely. He tied the cord off and went to work.

Gutting and skinning animals that he had killed was something Erik had done hundreds of times as an outdoorsman. This time was no different, aside for the raging anticipation for the meal he would soon be eating and the hindrance of his injured hand. Erik dumped the animal's innards on the empty sled and carried them far off into the brush where he dumped them. Slowly, he pulled the hide off of the young caribou. He then found the lighter and some of the remaining magazine paper and started a fire with some dry kindling.

Once the fire was roaring he continued to feed it, he wanted a nice thick bed of coals to cook with. The light that the fire gave off helped him see what he was doing and the small pocket knife, while not the best tool for the job, was working quite nicely. He slowly cut out the back straps and placed them on the sled. Same with the tenderloins, he then went to work cutting strips from the rump and back legs.

Erik then improvised a cooking spit with large rocks on each side of the fire. He found a green branch from a healthy tree that was an inch in diameter and shaved away all the bark. Sharpening the stick, he pierced it lengthwise through one of the back straps. Placing the ends of the stick on the taller rocks the meat was now over the bed of coals and began to slowly cook.

Figuring it was cold enough where the meat had no choice of spoiling, he went to work cutting more green branches for cooking. Soon he had several pieces of meat hovering over the coals at all angles.

The smell of the meat as it cooked was delightful and Erik could feel his mouth-watering. He soon ran out of patience and cut a strip off the original back strap. The fire licked at his hand and nearly set his cast on fire but he could not have cared less. He blew on the charred meat only a couple of times before he took a bite.

The richness and flavor of the meat were delicious and Erik decided that caribou must be the tastiest thing he had ever eaten. He consumed the piece quickly and went in to cut some more.

That is how Erik spent the rest of the night, feeding his fire, cooking his meat and eating. With no way to tell time, he was unsure of when he actually crawled into his sleeping bag. He only knew that his belly was full and he was warm and he was happy. The stars were sparkling and the fire crackling.

It was a good night's sleep.

# Chapter 24

When Canadian Elite Rescue pulled into the Watson Lake RCMP detachment station even Peter had to admit it was an impressive sight. Three of the younger officers quickly scurried to the window in the main office to watch the well-funded outfit as they arrived. Four brand new Ford F-150 pick-up trucks pulled into the station lot, the impressive CER logo on the doors. The trucks were impossibly clean and sharp looking and Peter wondered how they could have traveled down the dirty, dusty Canadian highways and still look so sharp.

"Look at this shit show," Ron mumbled under his breath.

"Yeah. It is what it is. Let's be smart and try to at least get the best use out of them that we can," Peter responded.

Peter was glad that Lauren was taking a walk in town at the moment. He did not want her to get her hopes up with the sight of this well-funded, but a poorly trained group. Besides, he had arranged a small surprise for her to make her feel more a part of the effort. He was still unsure why, but he felt a connection to her and admired her tenacity.

The front door to the station opened and in walked a short stocky man with a square jawline. His uniform was spotless and pressed and his boots had a high shine.

"Who's in charge here?"

"I am, Lt. Ron Jenkins. This is Sgt. McEwan, he is heading up rescue efforts."

"My name is Commander Lucas Emmerick, leader of the Canadian Elite Rescue team. By the way Lt., shouldn't you be using the term 'recovery' effort? Nobody survives over a week in this kind of terrain, especially after a plane crash."

Ron's neck and face reddened, "We don't like to call it a recovery effort until there is a body to recover, Commander. Besides we don't like to quit on people up here."

"Whatever. The prime minister himself ordered us up here to help you boys out. We have engagements elsewhere next week, so you have us for five or six days. Why don't you tell me what you have going on so far and tell me how my team can help? That is unless you want us to take charge?"

"Absolutely not!!" Peter said, his voice rising.

Winnie, ever loyal, had jumped from her spot on the sofa in front of the fire and was now at Peter's side. The hair on her spine began to stand and her muscles were tensed.

"We have a vested interest in seeing this through, we have a plan and we WILL be sticking to this plan. If you feel like you can't work alongside the RCMP than feel free to take your ass back to Edmonton."

Winnie was now letting out a low growl and was circling Commander Emmerick.

"Uhh. I think there is something wrong with your dog McEwan," the pompous Commander spoke.

"No, she just doesn't like assholes."

Sensing trouble, Ron stepped in.

"Enough of this bullshit!!! Commander, come

to my office and I'll bring you up to date on our search grids. Sgt. McEwan, make sure our boys have their grid maps and get them to the hangars to start today's search."

Peter quickly spun and left the room. It was going to be a real chore trying to coexist with these 'elite' guys. He tried to remind himself that any extra feet on the ground was a good thing and he didn't want Lauren to get the impression that the two groups could not get along.

The Sgt. instructed his three officers to go to the hangar with their updated search grids and join their pilots. As he sat in his office he hoped today would give them a lead. For only he and Ron knew the truth, today was the last day they could afford to pay the bush pilots to help in the search. All the air support funding was used up, they had even delved into next year's budget. After today they would have to rely on ground searches and that would be like searching for a needle in a haystack.

The wreckage needed to be found today.

Peter decided to let Ron work out the situation of how the CER could help. He and Emmerick had gone to Ron's office and it would take some time to get the new team up to speed. Meanwhile, Peter was going into town to find Lauren.

As he walked out of the station he passed the four trucks of the CER squad. All of the officers sitting in them appeared to be under thirty years old. There were a dozen of them, all clean-shaven and looking spiffy in their combat khakis and collared shirts with the logo on the chest. Peter couldn't even tell if he was jealous of them or angry with them. It wasn't their fault that they were mainly a political pet project. Peter wondered what he could accomplish with that team and their funding. What should have been a fine rescue force was being politicized and commanded by a clown.

Shaking his head, a frustrated Peter headed to Anita's diner to find Lauren. Winnie was hot on his heels, but first, she stopped to piss on the tire of one of the shiny CER trucks.

Peter smiled, "Good girl, Win."

# Chapter 25

The main street through Watson Lake was one of the few paved roads in town and Lauren walked along with it towards the diner. She took in the refreshing cold air as she walked and it helped her to clear her mind. Officer Marchont had worked his communications magic that morning and Lauren was able to speak with the boys. Young Evan was keeping up a brave demeanor but was missing his mother. Calvin was doing his best to be the man of the house but Lauren could tell he was emotionally spent.

Before saying goodbye she reminded them that she loved them and wherever their father was, he did too. She also made them a promise. She would be home in one week. Lauren knew she couldn't stay here forever, the boys needed her, and as much as she wanted closure it may not come.

Anita's diner was a rustic looking place, to say the least, and when Lauren entered she was a little nervous. There were perhaps a dozen patrons eating breakfast and she knew she probably stuck out like a sore thumb. In a town of this size, everyone knew one another.

"What can I get you dear?" asked a portly, native-looking woman.

"Just a cup of coffee, please."

The woman returned with a piping hot cup of joe.

"My name is Anita, this is my place. Anything you need you just tell me. We take care of people here and everybody in town is pulling for you, honey. Our home is your home."

A few people in the surrounding booths echoed her sentiment.

Lauren fought back tears, "Thank you so much. The men at the station have been bringing me food from here and I must say it is incredible. I must owe you something, please."

"Your money is no good here. You just warm up with that coffee and if you need anything to eat, or even someone to talk to, you let me know," the jolly woman responded.

Lauren brought the warm mug to her lips and took a sip. She welcomed the warmth it brought throughout her body. She picked up a newspaper off the counter and began to read. It was a copy of the Edmonton Journal and Lauren set herself to perusing it. She had been turning pages for a few minutes when she saw an article that caught her attention.

'Three missing in suspected Nahanni plane crash', read the headline. It was just a small article, near the back of the paper. It saddened Lauren that a moment that had changed her life forever was so small and insignificant to the rest of the world. Her sadness changed to guilt when she thought about it further. How many times had she read about a similar thing and shrugged it off as unimportant? She vowed to become a better, more caring person.

"Is this seat taken?"

Lauren was deep in thought and startled a bit. She turned to see Sgt. McEwan taking the stool next to her. He was clean-shaven and looked better rested than the previous night.

"Peter! You scared me. Please, sit down. Any news?"

Peter was careful to use caution when describing the 'help' that had arrived from Edmonton.

"Well, remember that elite rescue squad that Ron mentioned? They arrived this morning and are working with us now on some new search grids. Hopefully, we can have some feet on the ground by midday."

"Well that's good news, right," Lauren could sense that Peter was wavering.

"Sure, it's great news. The more men, the better. I just want you to understand, until we have a crash site we really don't have a starting point. We could have a thousand men on the ground; it is just a huge area we are trying to cover."

Lauren smiled, "But..... The more men, the better. Right?"

"Absolutely," Peter said, a grin crossing his own face.

"There are a dozen more men and they will be put to good use. Grab your coffee to go; I have something to show you."

"What is it, Peter?"

"Just come with me."

Lauren slyly put a twenty-dollar bill on the counter and said goodbye to Anita.

"We'll have a dinner sent over to the station for you dear, God bless you and your family."

"Thank you, Anita."

Lauren followed Peter to his truck and climbed in.  Winnie, who per the usual was impatiently waiting, instantly hopped onto her lap.

"Win, get down", snapped Peter.

"Oh leave her alone, she's keeping me warm," insisted Lauren.

Peter turned the ignition and pulled out of Anita's parking lot. The worn old government truck began to motor down the road.

"Are you going to tell me where we are going?"

"Well, I have arranged for you and I fly together today.  We will be covering our own search grid. My old friend Frank Atwater owes me a favor.  He runs a bush plane part-time and I helped him rebuild his barn after a big snowstorm caved in the roof last winter.  He is all fueled up and ready to go when we arrive."

"Oh, Peter! Thank you so much, you don't know what this means to me, to be able to actually see what we are up against. Thank you."

"Don't mention it. I'm happy to do it."

Frank owed no favor. Peter lied to Lauren; he had reached into his own pocket to pay for the plane that day. He had his reasons. Maybe, if Lauren saw how big and desolate the park was, she would be more realistic about the search. Also, he wanted to bring some happiness to a dark situation and if flying around the sky made Lauren happy he was glad to do it. This poor woman had a family to get back to and even though she deserved some closure she probably wouldn't be getting it.

"Here we are," Peter said after a few miles.

Lauren, Peter, and Winnie exited the old truck and walked to the hangar where they were greeted by Frank.

"Morning, Ma'am. Sgt. McEwan, I'm all ready to go when you are. Awful sorry 'bout the circumstances that bring ya up here Ma'am."

"Thank you, I'm just anxious to get up there and look around."

Soon all three were buckled in and taxiing down the short runway. Winnie was left behind in the hangar, much to her dismay. The plane gained speed, gently left the ground and soon was gaining altitude. Lauren was shocked at the beauty of the land the higher the little plane rose. Pine and spruce forest covered much of the area and she could see several small pristine lakes.

"Wow, it's very pretty down there."

"Yes, sometimes I forget what this place really looks like. It's easy to forget halfway through a tough winter, but up here in the sky it all looks.......so peaceful, I guess," Peter thoughtfully replied.

"We will be over the western part of the Nahanni in about fifteen minutes," Frank said over the hum of the spinning propellers.

After a few minutes, Peter broke the silence.

"So this trip to Scotland, when were you going to go?"

He felt stupid for asking and hated forced conversation but they were to be in the sky for the next few hours. They might as well kill some time.

"Mine and Erik's anniversary is next week.

Nineteen years. I was going to surprise him with a trip to Edinburgh. He is a history buff and wanted to see all the sights."

"My grandfather was born in Edinburgh," Peter responded. "He fought for the UK in World War 2. He was shot twice in the legs. When he got home he married my grandmother and settled near Inverness and worked as a stonemason. My dad always spoke of the beauty of the land and how I needed to see the Highlands with my own eyes. 'God's country', is what he called it. The same as most native people feel about this area, I suppose."

"Well, I can certainly see why. It's beautiful," Lauren stated.

"Erik often spoke about this trip and how the Territories were still largely wild and untamed. Now that I see it with my own eyes it's hard to describe," she continued.

"Over ninety percent of Canadians live within one hundred miles of the U.S. border. The few of us that live way up here like to consider ourselves the 'real' Canadians," Peter said, a large grin across his face.

Lauren laughed at this.

"Real wilderness folk, ehh? Still, it has to be a very hard life up here."

"Well, it is not the land of the overly sociable. As much as my sister pesters me to move back home I'm not really sure how I'd fit in. I've been living this isolated life for almost twenty-five years."

"You should do it, you know. You are still a young man. You could have a whole new 'part two' to your life. Nothing ventured, nothing gained, Peter."

He knew she was right. Family, a new job, new relationships, maybe even new romances were out there for him if he were only brave enough to take the first step.

"We'll see what happens, Mrs. Keller."

She smiled. Peter was a good man and deserved a chance at a new life, far from this isolated place. Natural beauty and devotion to job and country were great, but people need other people. It is, Lauren thought to herself, the very vein of human existence.

"We are crossing the South Nahanni River and entering our search grid now, Sgt. McEwan," Frank spoke from the cockpit.

Lauren looked to her left out the window and for the first time laid eyes on the mighty river. Huge valleys and gorges covered the land as if someone had dragged a huge ax through the middle of the wilderness. She was awestruck.

Peter explained the layout of the park, how the river split it in two from west to east. He described the four large valleys and how the last one held the incredible Virginia falls.

"Will we see it?"

"No", said Peter, "It's much further down and we suspect the crash site is in the western part of the park."

Lauren felt slightly guilty as if she were putting sightseeing in front of her real reason for being up there. Peter handed her a pair of binoculars.

"Now comes the fun part. Frank will fly north and south for five miles at a time turning one-half mile east before each turn. This is our grid. You have the left side and I have the right. It's going to seem mundane but this our best shot."

Lauren carefully adjusted her eyepiece and started looking down. It was all so beautiful but on the other hand, it all looked the same. The best they could do was try to find anything that stood out. Any shape or color that looked like it didn't belong.

Thus, the search began. For nearly two hours no one spoke as Frank flew back and forth over their grid. Lauren finally broke the silence.

"Peter, I feel like my eyes are crossed."

"Yes, I've done this a hundred times. When your eyes feel wonky just stare at a fixed object, like the floor of the plane for a few minutes. It will help you refocus your eyes. Either that or close your eyes and rest them for a moment."

Lauren didn't want to close her eyes. She did not want to chance missing something. Somewhere down there was Erik, the man she loved and joined her life with. She did not want to miss the chance to bring him home alive or otherwise. He deserved as much in her mind, for all of the devotion he had shown the boys and her. She must keep looking.

A few more hours ticked by and before they knew it the sun neared the horizon.

"Running low on fuel Sgt. Gotta head back in. Sorry Ma'am," Frank informed them.

Lauren looked forlornly out the window and

Peter thought she might cry. He still had to tell her, and before the night was over, that there was no more money for air searches. The ground searches were their only hope now. It was going to kill him to tell her, to watch her lose hope.

"Chin up, Mrs.Keller."

Lauren managed a weak smile as they headed back to Watson Lake. Thirty minutes later the plane was touching down on the runway. They landed safely and exited the plane. Peter fetched Winnie and was headed back to the truck with Lauren when an RCMP truck came roaring into the parking area. Young Marchont charged out of his vehicle and ran to Peter and Lauren.

"They found it sir!! They found it!! The plane, it's on the southwest side of a mountain in grid six. We have the coordinates. Lt. Jenkins wants you both back at the station so we can plan to drop ground parties at first light!"

"Yes!!" shouted Lauren as she hugged Marchont tightly, knocking his Mountie hat off in the process.

Peter let out a huge sigh of relief. He was off the hook and would not have to tell her that air support was over. But he did notice that

Marchont did not mention any signs of survivors. First thing tomorrow a crew would drop in and investigate.

By midday tomorrow Peter knew he would be delivering the body of Erik Keller to his grieving widow.

# Chapter 26

The air was cold and crisp when Erik awoke. Sharp pains rattled through his stomach and immediately he knew what it meant. With great difficulty, his body stiff from the hard ground, he rose quickly and left the camp in search of a tree.

Several minutes later, after some violent bowel movements, Erik returned to camp and sat on a rock. He was well aware of the problem. His body was caught off guard by the amount of food, and the richness of the meat, that he had taken in the previous night. Having not eaten much then gorging himself was more than his body could take, but he was feeling better now.

The small caribou, minus its hide, still hung from a branch and there was still plenty of meat on the skeleton. The cold air temperature kept the meat from spoiling but still, Erik had a decision to make. He could stay and eat as much as he could to strengthen his body for the remaining trip. He could set off now, leaving the remainder of the meat behind, or his last option. Figure out a way to travel with the meat.

After pondering his choices Erik decided on the latter. Smoking the meat over low heat would allow him to carry his food with him and delay the spoiling process. He had never smoked meat before but did have a general idea of how to do it. So Erik decided he would stay put for the day, hydrating, eating and prepping his food. He hated to lose a day of travel and his injuries were still a worry, but it was necessary.

Trekking along a now worn trail Erik went to the river bank to wash and fill his water once again. The Nahanni was roaring along at a quick pace and Erik was still stunned by its power and beauty. He had to be very careful when filling the water bottle that the force of the river didn't pull the bottle from his hands.

He drank two whole bottles and sat to tend to his wounds. The magazine cast was in poor shape having been soaked with rain and covered in blood from last night's butchering. Erik decided to pull it off as it was rotting away anyhow. Purple and green bruises covered his left hand and wrist but the swelling had subsided quite a bit. The pain, however, remained.

Next, he pulled the tube sock bandage from the gash on his shin. In the time since the crash, the wound had stopped bleeding but unfortunately, it was now an open seeping wound. The smell of infection and rotten meat overwhelmed him as he removed the bandage. Of all his ailments it was the shin wound that worried him most. If the infection moved into his bloodstream he was finished, he would be unable to travel.

Luckily, he had brought the bottle of whiskey along. He poured some generously onto the affected area and scrubbed it in with his last clean sock. The pain was incredible but he knew he had to do his best to fight the infection. Eventually, he had enough of the scrubbing and decided to leave the wound open to the air, at least for one day. Erik washed several pairs of bloody, dirty tube socks and collecting his things, returned to camp to dry the socks over the fire.

Stoking the still glowing embers in his stone circle he quickly brought the fire back to life. He spent the next hour collecting dried sticks and branches to feed his fire, enough to get him through the day and night.

From the time Erik was a child he had watched survival shows and camping documentaries. He remembered seeing a man smoking fish in the wild and thought the method the man used would work just as well for the caribou meat.

First, Erik used medium-sized stones to build a circle, not unlike the one for the fire. He then kept going, there was no shortage of rocks and stones, building a little silo type structure that was almost waist-high. To cover the silo he used the metal sled. He hated to chance ruining the little traveling companion but Erik figured he could carry his stores in his backpack for the remainder of his journey. Besides, he needed the smoker to have a flat top to let out as little heat as possible.

Erik then used sticks to transfer coals from the fire into the bottom of the smoker. He fed the coals until there was a fire; he then fed that fire until it cooked down into a pile of embers. Placing the metal lid back on, he tested it. After a few minutes, he removed the lid and felt the rush of heat flow upwards toward him.

The last thing he needed was smoke. He would accomplish this by adding wet branches and damp moss to the fire. Erik sharpened several sticks in the same fashion as a campfire marshmallow stick. Then he cut dozens of small strips of meat from the dead caribou. In order for the meat to cure the pieces must be as thin as possible and if all went well it would finish with a jerky-like texture.

Placing the meat covered sticks into the smoker, Erik added his wet fuel and placed the lid back on. Smoke instantly started billowing from holes in the stone walls of his little smoker. This was what he had hoped for. With no way to control the heat, the whole process would require a little trial and error.

Patience was not one of Erik's strong suits and after about thirty minutes he pulled the metal top aside and retrieved one of his sticks. The meat and the branch were charred black. Although he was disappointed, he had prepared for this. The fire was too hot and the meat stick holders to dry. Earlier Erik had prepared another bundle of skinned skewer branches and had left them soaking in the river tied together with paracord.

He cut more thin meat strips and placed them on the new, wet skewers. Removing about half of the coals from the smoker Erik then placed the sticks back inside. He fed the now smaller ember pile with wet moss and put the metal lid back atop.

*Less heat, more smoke.*

While he waited for the smoker to do its job Erik cooked small pieces of caribou on his open fire pit and ate. This is how he spent the remainder of his day, smoking meat, eating and occasionally napping. After his third attempt, he had figured the perfect ratio of heat versus time and the chewy jerky was coming out quite nicely.

As night approached Erik noticed storm clouds rolling in. He had finished smoking his last batch of jerky and decided the limited daylight would be best used collecting firewood and weatherproofing his camp. Using spruce boughs he covered his lean-to with an extra layer of weatherproofing. He even used some of the boughs to create a little mattress to improve his sleeping conditions.

Erik fed his fire until it roared. Then, under darkness, he pulled himself into his old sleeping bag. It had been a good day and he was happy with the work he had done. Tomorrow there would be time to get back to the real mission, getting home to his family. As he faded off to sleep Erik thought of his boys, visions of them playing Wiffle ball in the front yard made him smile.

He was just drifting off when the heavy rains came.

# Chapter 27

"Alright, alright!! Everyone calm down. One at a time please!!!" Lt. Ron Jenkins pleaded with the mob in his office.

Marchont had just returned to the RCMP station, along with Lauren and Peter. Commander Emmerick and a few of his crew had joined them in the main office, every one of them abuzz with the new information. Ron had managed to quiet them for a moment.

"We have a crash site and we have the coordinates. We need to have a definitive plan of action for tomorrow. Peter, I'd like you to lead the way. Do you have any thoughts?"

Everyone remained silent as Sgt. McEwan spoke.

"We need to drop a team tomorrow at first

light. If this is a recovery effort we should know immediately. The team will then extract all bodies from the site and do a thorough crash investigation."

His eyes flashed to Lauren at the mention of the word 'bodies'. She impressively remained steadfast and showed no emotion.

"In the case of survivors, we will make all efforts to airlift them as well. In the extreme case that we think someone has left the area alive, well......" Lauren and the rest of the men listened intently," I will make plans tonight for ground searches of the area. We need to acquire a chopper. Ron, where do we stand on that?"

Before the Lieutenant could speak Commander Emmerick cut in.

"I have made plans to bring our chopper in from Edmonton, it is on its way now and will be ready to go by morning."

Both Ron and Peter were obviously perturbed that the helicopter had not been brought in the day before, but both men were able to keep their anger under wraps. Even though he was disgusted with himself, Ron even managed to thank Emmerick.

"I'd like to lead the crash investigation and recovery tomorrow," the Commander continued.

"I'm going to remind everyone this is not a recovery yet, we will know more tomorrow," said Peter. He could see Emmerick roll his eyes.

"Commander Emmerick, you go ahead and lead the team tomorrow, it's your aircraft and your pilot," Ron spoke, "Everyone else, be here at daybreak."

With that everyone left the room with the exception of Peter and Lauren. Winnie joined Lauren and they both sat on the comfy sofa in front of the welcoming glow and warmth of the old wood stove.

"So...... tomorrow we will have some answers, right Peter?" Lauren's voice faded off as she stared at the stove.

"We will. Nobody knows what we'll find, so you keep your head up. Worst case tomorrow you will have no more worry. For now just promise me you will get some sleep," with that he headed for the door.

"C'mon, Winnie."

Peter looked back to see his old yellow Lab lying on the couch, her head on Lauren's lap. She was stroking Winnie's ears as she stared at the orange-bellied stove. She looked like a lost little girl and it pained Peter to see the doubt in her eyes. Lauren broke her gaze and looked at Peter.

"Can she stay?"

Peter looked at this broken woman whom he had known for less than a week, his own stomach turning at the thought of what tomorrow might bring.

"Absolutely. Good night ladies."

Peter shut the door and drove off into the night.

# Chapter 28

Lauren hardly slept that night.

After Peter left, she and Winnie sat on the couch for what seemed like hours. Eventually, she rose and went to the bunkroom where she showered. She wandered to the kitchenette in a zombie-like state, reheated some of sweet Anita's brisket and tried to eat. Her appetite failing her, she returned to the bunkroom where she laid down for the night. Winnie leaped up onto the bed beside her and curled up before dozing off.

Lauren's memories flooded her mind that night. She thought of her first meeting with Erik, a blind date set up by mutual friends. She was so busy with her studies that she almost didn't go. When she arrived and met Erik she was instantly swept in by his zest for life, his energy, his easy smile. Love at first sight? Maybe. She and Erik were never apart after that first night.

She thought of her pregnancy for Calvin. It was unexpected and very early in her and Erik's relationship. Great stress was upon both of them for the next nine months and neither knew if the budding romance could survive this curveball. But, when Calvin was born they became a family and she knew that Erik's devotion to them would never waver.

She thought of her wedding day, how handsome Erik looked in his tuxedo. She remembered the look in his eyes when she came down the aisle. She saw the love in his eyes and that the moment meant as much to him as it did to her.

She thought of all the years he worked the midnight shift so he could be home with the boys while she took classes or worked. How many evenings did she come home and find him passed out on the sofa, a sleeping toddler lying across his body and toys covering the living room floor?

She thought of the dreams they had shared all these many years, the trip to Scotland, a summer home by the ocean, watching two healthy successful boys finding their way through the world.

She thought, for the first time ever, of them sitting on a front porch. Impossibly old and holding each other's hand, enjoying their twilight. Together, as always.

She knew that the morning would likely bring cold truth but for now, for this one last night, she had her dreams intact and she would relish in them. Lauren fought sleep and thought of every good moment she had ever shared with her husband.

Last she looked at the clock it was 3:36 AM.

## Chapter 29

The rain was still coming down heavy when Erik stirred at first light. The extra work he had done on the lean-to had paid off and it was still relatively dry inside. He had the forethought to bring the packs in with him before he tucked in. Now he would have to prep for the coming days travel under his shelter.

Erik had also thought to bring his washed and dried tube socks inside with him. Now he set himself to wrapping his injured shin that he had left unprotected all night. The gash still looked infected but didn't smell as bad and Erik hoped the whiskey wash and fresh air did it some good.

The homemade cast was gone now, so Erik pulled three heavy socks over his left hand and wrist hoping to lessen any pain if he bumped it in his travels. He pulled out the better of the two raincoats; both were torn badly and pulled it on. Finding a filthy t-shirt at the bottom of one of the packs he tied it around his head in a turban-like hat. Lastly, he wrapped the beaten sleeping bag inside the other raincoat and forced it into one of his two packs. If the bag became wet it would make for a cold, hellish night and put his very survival at risk.

Before setting off he filled his last pack with the water bottle, leftover socks, his knife, the remaining fishing supplies and the smoked jerky he had made. Tearing a pocket from one of the raincoats he was able to fashion a little bag for the jerky. He hoped that he could get five days' worth of meals if he stretched it.

He used some sturdy sticks to fashion a frame and secured both packs to it. He made arm loops from the former straps of his sled and lifted it all on to his back. It wasn't that heavy he thought, but slightly awkward. He was hopeful it wouldn't affect his balance or snag on limbs and bushes. He kicked wet earth onto the remaining coals in the fire pit and headed off, his gun at his hip.

After finding the riverbank, Erik was thrilled at the time he was making. The terrain was mostly flat and he was able to keep within sight of the river for the most part. He figured that he must be in one of the plains areas that were situated between the large canyons that directed the powerful river. The rain had stopped and the wildlife was emerging from the pine forest. Several squirrels crossed his path and he watched several types of hawks circling the sky, searching for prey. By midday, he figured he had covered up to five miles.

Erik perched on a large flat rock next to the river. Dropping his pack to the ground, he lay down on his back and stared at the emerging sun. He stayed that way for some time until an unfamiliar noise rattled his senses.

Sitting upright and cocking his head, he listened carefully. The sound started off as a small hum and slowly grew louder. Erik tried his best to assign the sound to something.

It was a plane!!!

The sound he heard was the hum of propellers. Erik sprang up and tried to spot the source of the sound. The skies were still partly overcast and although he searched the skies for a few minutes he could not locate the plane.

As quickly as the sound came, it went away. This did not dampen Erik's spirits though, in fact, it buoyed them. Civilization was that much closer and though he had no way of knowing if it were a search plane or just some bush pilot ferrying passengers, to him it was a sign of hope.

Erik pulled two pieces of jerky from his bag and ate them, washing it down with cold, clean Nahanni water. Yes sir, it was a great sign, he thought to himself. Happily, he pulled his pack back on and headed off once more along the banks of the mighty river.

# Chapter 30

It was still very early when people started to arrive at the Watson Lake RCMP detachment. The energy was high and everyone was eager to get to work. Lauren and Winnie were there to greet each Officer with a smile and a cup of coffee and the general feeling around the station was one of tempered optimism.

"Alright everyone, listen up," announced Lt. Jenkins, "In fifteen minutes the CER chopper will be leaving. A team led by Commander Emmerick will airdrop into the nearest clearing they can find. Due to the wreckage being located on a series of steep ridges we will have to drop the team approximately one and ¾ miles southwest of the crash site. Four men will accompany the

Commander, two from the CER and two from RCMP. Once the site is reached any survivors or wounded would be the first priority. After the recovery of any deceased, a crash investigation will take place. Commander Emmerick, are your men and the chopper ready to go?"

"They are Lieutenant."

"Officer Marchont has worked some communications magic with a radio tower in Fort Laird. The rest of us here will be able to listen to, and have conversations with, the team in Nahanni," Lt Jenkins continued," O.K. then, fall out."

With that, all the men began to scurry to their assigned posts. Peter and Lauren would be listening in as they looked over topographical maps of the area. Various RCMP officers would be stationed on road duty and some in Fort Laird to arrange flights for any injured survivors that may be found.

"Officer Marchont, we need to talk to you," Lt Jenkins said, as he and Peter pulled the young officer aside.

"You will be dropping in with Emmerick," Peter instructed him.

"But sir, I don't have a lot of field experience. I'm mostly communications and PR, you know that."

"Listen," Ron interrupted," You've been trained. You can handle it. We need one of our own on the site, someone we can trust. I don't want Emmerick to manipulate the findings. He is a glory hound and would say anything to promote his team. It's probably just me being paranoid, but I want one of my men there and Peter wants to be here to support Mrs. Keller."

Marchont stood tall as he spoke," I understand Lt. You can count on me sir."

Within fifteen minutes the shiny white helicopter with the red CER insignia lifted off for the seventy-minute flight to the crash site. Peter and Lauren set themselves up at the map station in the office. Winnie took up her usual residence in front of the woodstove.

"Listen," Peter said to Lauren, "These landing parties can take some time reaching their location. Even then communications and feedback can be spotty. Try to be patient and relax, I know it's not easy."

"I'm O.K., Peter. I have waited this long, I can

handle a few more hours."

A light rain began to fall and the two of them nursed a pot of coffee as they waited. Two hours later came the first communication with the landing team. It was Officer Marchont's voice reporting in.

"We have found the wreckage site at the coordinates given. Our chopper hovered over the sites as Commander Emmerick took photos. There appear to be two large sections of the plane sitting on separate ridges about 200 yards apart."

"What does that mean?" Lauren whispered to Peter.

"Shhh. Wait until he is done."

Marchont continued, "We have found a clearing south of the site and will be dropping in shortly. Will report back ASAP."

The radio went silent and Peter tried his best to soothe Lauren.

"Two pieces of wreckage is not a bad thing. Not to be graphic, but if there was a direct impact with a mountainside there would be no large parts of the aircraft left intact. Any large sections of the plane we see tell us that there was likely glancing impact. Still, please don't let this give you false hope. I...."

Lauren cut him off, "I know, I know......I'm still mentally prepared. Please don't worry. I'm ready for any news they send us."

Before long Marchont was reporting again, by now Ron had joined Lauren and Peter at the communications/map station, hot cup of java in hand.

"We are on the ground. We found a suitable landing area. I repeat all five of us and equipment are now on the ground. We will now begin the ascent of the ridge. Approximately three thousand feet up to the site. I will report back when we reach it."

"It will take them more than an hour to cover that distance," Ron stated.

"An hour," Lauren whispered to herself.

In an hour she would learn the fate of her husband. She would have to report home to the family and make arrangements. In one hour her world was likely to change forever and she was unsure if she could handle it.

For the past week, she had been in this beautiful but lonely place. The people here were wonderful and perhaps under different circumstances, she would have loved her stay. Unfortunately, her week in Watson Lake was a living hell, her time spent waiting for word of a dead spouse. Only the men of the RCMP and sweet Winnie made it bearable.

She drank coffee as she waited, too scared to even leave the desk area. Ron and Peter had left a few times to speak privately in Ron's office. Every passing minute was torture. The hour mark came and went. They were well into their second hour of waiting when Peter finally tried to reach the team.

"Base to Marchont. Status report."

"Marchont on, ground team reads you loud and clear base."

"Where are we, Marchont?"

"We have reached the wreckage on the lower ridge. Two of us are investigating here. Commander Emmerick and two others are climbing to the upper ridge wreckage. We have what appears to be the back half and one wing of the plane here. No deceased or injured found here as of yet. Will continue searching area. Stand by."

Lauren's heart was beating fast inside of her chest. Peter and Ron anxiously sat on the edge of their chairs. Peter was starting to regret not going along with the team. Another twenty minutes passed by. The radio crackled to life, this time it was Emmerick's voice.

"Commander Emmerick to Base"

"We hear you, team leader," replied Ron.

"We have reached the upper ridge wreckage site. We have two confirmed deceased at this time. One positive identification of Gus Atkins, confirmed from driver's license in wallet. No I.D. on the second deceased of yet. Appears to be male, over 6 ft in height. Blonde hair....."

"Oh my God, that's John. Oh my poor friend..." Lauren was overcome by emotion. Tears tracked down her cheeks. For all of the worry over her husband she had all but forgotten John Woodsley. He was like an older brother to her and her children adored him.

"Only two deceased so far?" Peter broke in.

"At this time. Investigation incomplete. Will be in contact."

This is going to make things complicated, Peter thought to himself.

Lauren was barely holding on and if Erik's body wasn't located it would open up a Pandora's box. A body from an air crash could be anywhere on that mountainside. There was even an outside possibility that he could have bailed out before the crash. Would she be able to leave without answers?

"I have made some calls ahead to Fort Laird. Our boys up there will receive the bodies and see them to the morgue. Once autopsies are performed we will release them to their families. I'm sorry about your friend Mrs. Keller," Ron said.

"Thank you."

Lauren had been in brief contact with John's ex-wife. John was somewhat estranged from her as well as his teenage daughter. Both had moved to Michigan after the ex remarried. Both of John's parents had passed and his siblings were scattered across the country. There was a very good chance that Lauren would be arranging not one, but two funerals.

What followed next was an extremely tense hour of no communication. Peter was adamant to both Ron and Lauren that the ground crew be left alone to finish their work. Eventually, it was Commander Emmerick who broke the silence.

"Team leader to base. Crash recovery and

investigation complete. We will be returning to our original drop point to clear rocks and brush for a landing. We will be returning to Fort Laird with two deceased, flight logs and a few personal items. I repeat, only two bodies recovered. Will be returning to Watson Lake before dark for debriefing. Team leader out."

Back in Watson Lake, Lauren and the men sat in silence for some time. It appeared that Lauren Keller would be traveling back to the states with no body and no answers and this made no one happy. Peter, as well as the rest of the detachment, felt horrible. They had all grown fond of Lauren during her stay and admired her spirit and devotion.

Lauren excused herself from the room and Ron and Peter went to their respective offices. They would all wait for the debriefing and then the men would see that Lauren Keller's flights were in order. It was the least they could do.

In front of the big wood stove, Winnie was left alone, she circled twice before lying down and she quietly began to whine.

# Chapter 31

It was mid-afternoon when Erik was hit with another obstacle. The bank along the river had grown steep and he was forced to hike away from it. Before long he was facing another tall ridge, perhaps the beginning of another one of the giant valleys that were carved by the South Nahanni River. He was left with a decision to make, camp for the night or press onward.

The last time he was forced to camp atop a ridge he nearly froze to death in his little stone tomb, but this day was different. It was much warmer and clear and he was well fed and energized. He decided to go forward and climb.

This particular incline was not as steep as the one he had encountered days before, but it was much higher. Without the sled pulling behind him he was finding the climb easier and by dark had traversed the entire ridge and now sat at the top looking down. It was easy to be mesmerized by the view of the mighty river carving its way through the valley below. Erik could see far down the river from his perch, maybe as far as five miles. Once he was down off of the ridge he could see it was relatively flat for quite a distance and this boosted his spirits even more.

Each day he was gaining confidence that he might actually make it out of the Nahanni alive and hold his wife and boys again. During the day his struggles to survive and keep moving kept him on point, but at night was when he missed his family the most. Tonight would be another of those lonely nights.

*Don't give up on me yet.*

It was time to set up camp and trees and branches were scarce at his extreme elevation. Like the last cold, miserable night he spent on top of a ridge he would have to build a stone fort. Again, rocks and stones were everywhere, so Erik began by finding two boulders that were close together and started stacking rocks behind them to make a back wall. Unlike the previous stone fort he no longer had the metal sled for a roof.

Fortunately, the wind was not blowing and there was no precipitation to speak of. Erik's roof this night would be the worse of his two raincoats held in place by rocks. The coat didn't cover the whole shelter but Erik was confident that it would at least hold in some of his body heat. It would have to work because there would be no fire for lack of fuel.

By the time darkness settled in Erik was snuggled tight in his fort buried deep in his trusty sleeping bag. The temperature was near forty and it was one of the warmer nights he had endured during this whole ordeal. He was thankful that he didn't have to battle the elements for at least one night.

Tomorrow was a new day and he hoped to gain even more ground on his return to the world. The last thing he thought of before he fell asleep is that he definitely found what he came to Canada to find.

Adventure.

# Chapter 32

The mood was somber as everyone started to gather at the Watson Lake RCMP station. Nearly all of the officers were back with the exception of the five from the helicopter/ground crew. Lauren sat on the sofa with Winnie, wrapped in a blanket, drinking a cup of coffee. Peter and Ron were busy putting away topographical maps and typing reports on the recovery effort. Everyone was ready for this ordeal to be over.

"They're here," said Lt. Ron Jenkins.

Peter turned to see two white pick-up trucks filled with CER team members roll into the station parking lot. They all entered the station and headed to the main office, Commander Emmerick leading the way. Peter and Ron joined them, Lauren trailing behind still wrapped in her blanket.

"Does she really need to be here for the debriefing?" asked Emmerick.

"She's been here all along and she will stay until we are done," snapped a tired and irritated Lt. Jenkins.

"Where are our two RCMP men from the recovery crew?" Peter chimed in.

"They were behind us, they'll be here shortly. Let's wrap this up now, nobody wants to be here."

Emmerick started the debriefing. He went on to explain the difficulty of the landing site, how the men repelled down. He talked about the climb and the finding of the wreckage. Lastly, he discussed the recovery of the two bodies and how the team carried them down the mountain, cleared a landing space and loaded the chopper.

The entire debriefing was all being recorded; it made the CER team sound heroic and exemplary without even mentioning the two accompanying RCMP officers.

"Any questions?" asked Emmerick.

"Do we have any indication as to what caused the accident?" asked Ron.

"No. the weather reports from that night show no unusual weather. Until the autopsies and toxicology reports come back we are leaning towards pilot error."

Peter was next, "Any thoughts on the unrecovered third passenger?"

Emmerick sat silently for a moment and seemed reluctant to keep talking. Lauren sat close by with a tense look on her face and an eerie confusion filled the room.

At that moment Officer Marchont burst into the office, moving at top speed and shouting as he entered.

"Did I not specifically ask that you wait for my return, Commander?!?"

Marchont's face was red, his fists clenched as he approached the Commander. Both Peter and Ron were startled, as neither had seen Marchont angry before.

"What have you told them so far," the young officer directed his question to Commander Emmerick.

"Step back son, you're talking to a commanding officer!!" Emmerick shouted as he jumped to his feet, his chair toppling over.

"What in the hell is going on here?" Peter demanded.

"Everyone shut the fuck up, now!!" Ron ordered. "Sit down and be quiet. If you can't do that, leave this office."

Order was restored temporarily, only the uncharacteristically furious Marchont remained standing.

"Now, Officer Marchont," Ron said, "What has got you so wound up?"

Marchont stood silent for a minute as he tried to gather himself. Still, his voice shook as he began to speak.

"Footprints, sir?"

"Footprints? What do you mean?"

"Sir, I found two partial footprints over seventy yards from the wreckage."

Commander Emmerick leaped from his seat again, "Christ Jenkins, those could be from a goddamn hiker!!"

"At that height?!? With no hiking trail??" Peter questioned.

"I also found a small smear of blood on a large boulder next to the wreckage. The wreckage on the lower ridge.....where NO bodies were found," stated Marchont.

"What exactly are you saying, Marchont?"

asked Ron.

The entire room was now silent, everyone was either standing or on the edge of their seats. Lauren had dropped her blanket as she stood at Ron's side.

"Sir, Commander Emmerick disagreed with me at the wreckage site as he does now. But, it is my belief that Erik Keller survived the initial impact and headed down that mountain. The footprints and blood at the lower wreckage site cannot be explained any other way."

"Even if he did survive a goddamn animal has probably dragged him away by now!!" screamed Emmerick.

That was more than Ron Jenkins could take. He jumped across the table, striking Emmerick hard in the jaw with his right fist. What followed was a mad scramble of CER and RCMP officers knocking over desks and chairs as they pulled their two commanding officers apart. Peter had to grab Winnie by the collar to keep her from jumping into the melee.

"You goddamn asshole! You aren't going to speak like that in my station with this woman sitting here. She's been through enough without hearing your shit!" Ron shouted, all of his pent up anger released at once.

"I'll have your job for this!!" yelled Emmerick, blood running from his lips.

"Take it! There's nothing you can do to me. I could have retired years ago!"

"The Prime Minister will hear about this!!"

"ENOUGH!!" Peter yelled," Get your man out of here, now."

With that, the CER team members led Emmerick out of the station. They loaded into their white trucks and tore from the parking lot. Ron retreated to his office, slamming the door behind him. The remaining RCMP Officers all went to their respective offices, only Peter, Lauren and Marchont remained.

Peter spoke first.

"Kid, are you a hundred percent sure about this?"

Marchont looked at Lauren, stood tall and tried to straighten his now torn uniform shirt.

"Sgt. McEwan, I am absolutely positive that Mr. Keller survived that wreck."

Peter placed his hand on Marchont's shoulder.

"Good job, Officer."

Lauren, tears flowing down her face, approached Marchont. Reaching up, she wrapped both arms around his neck and kissed him on the cheek.

"My Hero," she whispered.

Young Officer Marchont nodded, spun on his heels and left the room, a huge smile upon his face.

The room was a disaster area, papers, and chairs everywhere. The events that had unfolded were unexpected and left all involved emotionally spent. Lauren turned silently towards Peter, her blonde hair a mess, her eyes red. She looked confused, unsure that what she just heard and witnessed was real.

"Peter..... What now?"

"Now Lauren, we are going to go find your husband."

# Chapter 33

Erik woke to the sound of a hawk screeching. It was cold, but not unbearably cold. He rubbed his eyes and rolled to his side and instantly felt something wrong. His leg, the one with the gashed shin, was on fire and pain shot all the way up to his hip.

Erik also noticed that despite the cold, he was sweating profusely. Pulling his torn pant leg to the side he inspected his injury. His leg was grotesquely swollen and smelled horrible, like rotten meat. The thing that he had worried most about was now a reality. The infection in the leg wound had entered his bloodstream.

*Shit, this is not good.*

His timeline for rescue had just dramatically sped up. Forget about food and water, he was becoming seriously sick. It was doubtful that he could make it more than a couple of days if the infection progressed rapidly.

Now faced with this new obstacle, Erik was determined to do every task at double time. He quickly grabbed the bottle of whiskey from his pack and scrubbed the wound. He felt no shame as he loudly screamed in pain. Grabbing two of the cleaner tube socks he wrapped his shin. Placing the top back on the whiskey, and noticing it was now only a quarter full, he returned it to the backpack.

Erik returned the raincoat/roof and all other gear into the packs, attached them to the wooden frame he had assembled, and headed down off the ridge. He wasted no time enjoying the view this time. The descent off of the ridge and down to the river bank was much steeper than the trip up. Erik used rocks and boulders as steps, lowering himself slowly and at times sliding on his rear. It was slow going but he needed to reach the river as fast as possible. His body needed water, and lots of it, to fight off the infection.

By mid-morning Erik found himself once again at the foot of the South Nahanni River. His leg continued to throb and any time he put weight on it he was in a great deal of pain. Finding a large flat boulder, Erik sat down and drank from his refilled water bottle. Even though he wasn't hungry at all, he forced himself to eat a few pieces of his caribou jerky.

Since finding the South Nahanni River he had climbed up, and back down, two giant riverside ridges. By his own rough estimation, he had traveled about twenty-five miles along the river. Erik knew that the Nahanni cut through four large valleys before exiting the mountains or reaching any villages. He also knew that the last of these canyons would be unmistakable because it contained the enormous Virginia Falls.

That meant he had at least one more canyon to climb and even after that, another twenty miles or so before he had any chance of finding a road. It was a daunting task and Erik decided the only chance he had was to put it in the back of his mind and press forward.

After a short rest, he forced himself to his feet and started once again along the riverside. The land he was traveling in was mostly flat and he was able to move quickly along the bank by walking on the larger boulders. His thoughts were more focused now and there was less daydreaming. There was also less feeling sorry for himself and worrying about his family. There was only Erik and the river that guided him.

It was because of this focus that he nearly got himself killed.

Jumping down off of a boulder he looked ahead to see three huge Grizzly bears fishing in the stream. They were no more than thirty yards away and noticed Erik immediately. The largest raised his nose to the air and began to sniff. The smell of Erik's unwashed body and infected leg must have been completely obvious to the predators.

For a moment neither man nor beast moved. Then, very slowly, the bears grouped together and started to approach Erik. For a moment he froze, then remembering his sidearm he drew the Glock from its holster. He raised it and directed it at the bears.

"YAHH!!! SHOOO!!!! Get the hell out of here!!" he screamed.

This only served to frighten the animals and their approach quickened. Erik pointed the gun at the stones in front of the bear's feet and fired three shots.

BANG! BANG! BANG!

The sounds of the gun firing made even Erik jump as the sounds echoed through the river banks. Small pieces of stone sprayed up at the bears and two of them quickly spun and retreated for the woods. The largest stopped only for a moment before standing tall on his back legs and letting out a hair tingling roar.

Erik kept the gun locked on the animal and waited. The bear returned to all fours, waited for a second or two, and then broke into a fast trot towards Erik. With no time to overthink the situation he simply reacted to the threat. He fired three more times, his gun kicking violently in his right hand.

The bear was hit at least once and shrieked in pain. It turned, doubled over in pain, and ran into the trees in the same direction the other two had fled. By now Erik's heart was beating fast and he began to feel light-headed. He sat down, filled his bottle and took a drink.

Overwhelmed with what had just happened, he sat there on the rocks for a few moments. After the shock wore off he was unsure what to do. Following the river bank meant he would be heading in the general direction that the bears had just run to and he could possibly encounter them again. He felt some guilt shooting the animal, it was just being itself in nature, but he had to protect himself as well.

Erik realized he had no choice but to press on down the river, bears or no bears. He could not turn back, where would he go back to? After taking another drink, and with much trepidation, he returned to his journey.

He had endured a plane crash, injuries, freezing temperatures and now bears. What obstacle would the Nahanni throw at him next?

## Chapter 34

A newly re-energized Peter was now in his office putting the final touches on a ground rescue plan. It was two o'clock in the morning and he was running on adrenaline and coffee. This new information had placed him in the very spot he thrived on, ground search and rescue.

Every one of the Watson Lake officers had been instructed to return to the station before daybreak. Peter placed a call to the Fort Laird RCMP station on the east side of the Nahanni. He explained the situation of a possible crash survivor to the Lieutenant in charge and the commanding officer pledged four of his officers to the search. He told Peter he was no fan of the pompous CER and laughed aloud at the telling of Lt. Ron Jenkins punch.

Peter had kept Lauren up until well past midnight grilling her for more information. He wanted to know exactly how well Erik was educated on the Nahanni Park. Was he really a capable outdoorsman? Did he have real survival skills, could he tell direction? How fit was he?

By the time he sent her off to the bunkroom for some sleep, he knew this much. Erik Keller was a tough son of a bitch. He had worked in a maximum-security prison for many years. He worked out three times a week. He was reasonably fit, hunted, hiked and was an avid outdoorsman. He also had a wonderful wife and two young sons to return to.

Most importantly Lauren told Peter about the stack of books on Northern Canada, and specifically the Nahanni, that Erik had read and studied. There was no doubt that he was well prepared. What Peter did not know was the extent of Erik's injuries. Was he able to keep moving, able to hike the rough terrain? Did he have any food or cold weather gear?

In the end, Peter decided there was a very small chance that this guy could make it out and that was enough for him. Peter fell asleep at his desk, his head resting on a map of the Nahanni.

A couple of hours later he was awakened by

Lauren opening his office door.

"Peter, you awake?"

He opened his blurry eyes, "Yeah, what time is it?"

"Its 5:45, everybody is arriving and ready to go."

"O.K. Give me a minute."

It was showtime. Did Peter have one more miracle up his sleeve? What he hadn't told a soul was that this was it for him; he was done after this case. He'd had his fill. Between the politics, the CER, his age and the emotion of this case, he was done. He was going to retire.

But before he was done he was damn well going to find Erik Keller, dead or alive.

Peter exited his office, a hot cup of coffee in hand. The main office was filled with all of the RCMP officers, a few Fort Laird officers and to Peters's surprise, Commander Emmerick and two of his cronies. Everyone was silent and all eyes were on Peter.

"Alright everybody listen up. Lt. Jenkins has excused himself from command and I'm calling all the shots from here on in. I have devised a plan to search the area north of the Nahanni River. Don't ask how but we have managed to scrape up enough funds to get helicopters to airdrop two teams and retrieve us at the conclusion of our search."

"Make it three copters and three teams," interrupted Commander Emmerick, speaking through swollen lips.

"Commander?" Peter asked, surprised.

"We are going to stay on the case. The CER will not leave here with a man possibly alive out there, regardless of how unlikely it is to find him."

Peter thought about it for a minute before burying his pride.

"Very well Commander, I've got just the right job for you and your men."

Emmerick gave a nod to him and Peter continued.

"Based on the information we have attained from the crash site, and from what Mrs. Keller has told me, we have a possible survivor who is very familiar with the topography and waterways of the park. Based on the location of the crash site, I think Mr. Keller is headed south. First off, the direction down from the wreckage puts him south and into a valley that runs north and south.

Secondly, regardless if he even knows where he was at the time of the crash, he will know that heading south does one of two things. It leads him straight down to the highway to Watson Lake or straight down to the Nahanni. Now, we have the luxury of knowing what he doesn't. The exact site of the crash location. It is my belief that he will go to the South Nahanni River and head east, as it is the surest way to civilization. Does anyone disagree with this assessment?"

No one spoke and every person in the room was showing Peter their full attention.

"Good. We have one shot at this. We do not have the manpower to cover large areas so we will concentrate on three small areas. We have to hope we guess right. The Fort Laird contingent will airdrop twenty miles west of the crash site and follow the Nahanni due east on the off chance our survivor decided to go that way. Commander Emmerick will take most of his men and a few RCMP officers back to the crash site. They will split into two teams and search every square inch on the south side of that mountain. Its only ten miles south to the Nahanni river from the wreckage and I want every bit of that area searched for footprints, campfires, anything that looks like it could have come from our survivor. Commander, any thoughts?"

"No, Sergeant, carry on."

"Finally, I will drop in across from Virginia Falls on the north side of the river and head west. Even a healthy man could not have made it that far in the time since the crash, and our man is likely to have injuries. I will take three CER men with me. Our entire search is a gamble and based on the hope of our man reaching the river. If he was too hurt to make the river I have confidence Commander Emmerick's team will locate him. Any questions?"

After a few moments of silence, Peter continued.

"I've thought about this a great deal", Peter looked at Lauren as he spoke, "We have four days. We have exhausted all of the resources we have and the fact that we have found the wreckage so late and are just starting the ground effort, well.......We have to be realistic. This is our last shot and it's a long shot."

Lauren gave Peter a nod of understanding. She knew that even now it was unlikely Erik was alive. She was thrilled at the news Marchont brought and was grateful to all involved, even the CER. Peter had carefully explained to her that night that it was very doubtful an injured man could navigate the Nahanni. He didn't tell her that he thought Erik might be dead already. The weather had recently turned colder and it did not bode well for an injured man traveling on foot in the mountains.

"Fort Laird team and my team, you have one hour to pack tents, cold weather gear, food, weapons, anything you will need for four days in the park. Keep in mind we want to travel fast and light to make the best time possible. We will be heading out at 7 am. Commander Emmerick, your team can stay on the ground or return each night. It's your chopper and your fuel."

"I presume we will be staying on the ground until the conclusion of the search, Sergeant."

"One last thing. Officer Marchont will be running all communications right here at our station. All teams will be equipped with two-way radios and extra batteries. It's easy to get lost in the Nahanni. That is all; forward all information from this point on to Marchont in the command center. Good luck, men."

Every person left the office at that point knowing their assignment at the very least. Marchont sat in the main office at his communications center, maps and radios ready to go. Lauren walked Peter to the door, Winnie close behind them both.

"Good luck, Peter," she said, giving him a hug," I know that you have pulled out all the stops. Thank you and good luck."

"Of course, Lauren. Hope for the best. I'll be in touch."

Before they closed the door Lauren dropped to her knees and kissed Winnie on the nose.

"Good luck girl, stay safe."

Winnie's tail wagged with delight all the way to the truck.

# Chapter 35

Erik had continued his trek along the river since his encounter with the bears, but with much more caution. He couldn't afford any more surprises. His leg was causing him a great deal of pain but he tried to keep his mind clear. The sun was going down and he would have to make camp soon.

He had to decide to make camp by the river or in the woods. Wildlife, more specifically predators, was more likely to be near the water but Erik decided that he could not waste the energy to walk into the forest. He would have to set up camp right where he was.

The weather was clear but the temperature had dropped considerably. Erik also decided to make a simpler camp than some of his previous shelters; this afforded him a chance to save as much energy as possible. Searching the river bank he found a nice crevasse between two large boulders just feet from the river. He found some smaller dried logs washed up on the bank and placed them over the rocks and topped it with both raincoats. He unrolled his sleeping bag, stretched out and tried to force some caribou meat down.

He was nauseous from the fever and could eat only a few bites. Erik decided to have a very small fire, just enough to warm himself before he slept. He gathered as many small branches and twigs as he could and made a small circle of stones. Again, he had no trouble starting his fire.

The stars were out now and being on the bank of the river there were no trees to block his view. He sat by the small fire and warmed his body as he rubbed his sore thighs. His fever had not gotten any worse but it certainly wasn't getting any better either.

As the fire died down Erik took one last drink from his water bottle and pulled himself deep into the tattered sleeping bag. He wasn't uncomfortable but his body was on the brink of exhaustion. Regardless, he could not sleep. He lay there wondering if this day or the next might be his last on Earth.

For the first time, he questioned his own mortality. He was not afraid though, he was at peace with the decision to push himself right to the brink of death if it meant reuniting with his family. Eventually, he fell asleep to the sound of the river rolling on by.

He was unsure how long he had been sleeping when he was startled awake. What was it he heard? He lay awake, listening. For a while there was no sound other than the river. Then, loudly and very close by, he heard the sound again.

It was howling. The howling of wolves.

Erik knew there were wolves in the Nahanni National Park but last he'd read their numbers were dwindling and sightings were scarce. But here he was, and there was no doubt in his mind what he had heard. It was definitely Timberwolves and they were nearby.

Erik now regretted not building a larger fire as he lay still in his bag. Quickly, he went through his mind and counted the remaining bullets left in his pistol. One shot at a caribou early in his ordeal, two at the caribou he had killed, six at the bears.

Nine shots total. That meant he had five left. Five shots left to defend himself for the rest of his possibly short life.

Erik slept no more that night; instead, he sat there with his gun in hand, waiting for daylight.

# Chapter 36

It had been a few hours since Peter and his team of three CER guys had been airdropped next to the South Nahanni River. He had not laid eyes on the majestic Virginia Falls in some time but it still took his breath away when they flew over. None of the CER team members had ever seen its grandeur and there was a bit of muffled 'ooing and ahhing' from the back of the chopper.

They had repelled from ropes into a clearing and Peter gave instructions immediately. The team would cover 100 yards from the river and head due west. Every twenty-five yards a man would be stationed, Peter having the section closest to the river. The men would then proceed parallel to each other, and report any findings.

The highest-ranking of the CER men was Sgt. Timmons, but Peter did not recognize his rank as he didn't believe any of them were qualified to call themselves officers.

"Timmons, I'll take the riverbank, you will be twenty-five yards off my flank with your guys to your right. Keep them all in line and as even as possible. We are going to move quickly. Report anything unusual, as small as it may be."

"Yes, sir."

With these instructions, the ground search was underway. There was a reason Peter had decided to comprise his small team with the CER men. He didn't think they could be trusted and he wanted as many of his men as possible with Emmerick's team to report any findings the Commander might see as trivial.

Instructions were given to keep the radio channel as free as possible and only report on movements and findings. Each team was also told to send their GPS coordinates to Marchont every two hours so he could track them on his maps and make sure they hadn't wandered too far off course. A full assessment report would be radioed in at seven PM each night, other than that Peter wanted as little radio traffic as possible.

Virginia Falls was located in the fourth, and final of the giant canyons that the mighty river flowed through. Peter and his team found themselves climbing one of these canyons almost immediately. The climbing was tough and Winnie led the way. The three team members were holding their own and even showed some climbing and rope skills. By midday, they had reached the top of the ridge looking down at the river. It was an awesome sight and Peter was not even irritated when the guys pulled out their phones to take photos.

He radioed in his coordinates to Officer Marchont and when he was done he asked him to put Lauren on the radio.

"Hello? Peter?"

"Lauren, this is Sgt. McEwan," he was mindful to be professional as it was a party line, "I just want you to know that all three teams are on the ground and off to a good start."

"Thank you, and please everyone, stay safe."

"We will. I will talk with you tomorrow, over and out."

It must be hell for her to sit and wait for our

reports, Peter thought to himself.

Lauren had made it this far and he was confident she would be able to see this through. It wouldn't be long now; soon they would all have their answers.

Peter's team was done eating and hydrating and it was time to get moving.

"Alright, men, let's move out!"

If Peter could say nothing else decent about the men of the Canadian Elite Rescue, he could say this. They followed orders well. At no time did he hear any negativity or grumbling from Emmerick's men. He figured they were all happy to be doing some real work, not just going to a political rally or showing up at the end of some tragedy to take credit for someone else's work.

The team now climbed down off of the ridge. They made better time, but the terrain was just as dangerous. Many times one of the men would place his feet against a rock, using it as an anchor, only to have it give way and tumble far down below. This was a rough territory and Peter was mindful to relay that information to his team.

By late afternoon they were back to flat ground and making decent time along the river bank. As he walked along the rocky bank Peter began to put himself In Erik's place. How would he be proceeding? How would he shelter at night? These thoughts always seemed to help Peter in ground searches. What appeared obvious to a trained officer may not be as clear to an injured, scared, or lost individual. It was important to see things from a different perspective.

Peter was hoping to cover fifteen to twenty miles a day, a tall order in this wild country. From the crash site to the Nahanni was over ten miles and it was nearly eighty more to Virginia Falls. If Erik Keller was able to find the Nahanni River and was smart enough to keep to it in an eastern direction, Peter might find him. Assuming Erik was hurt and made about five miles a day, with Peter making fifteen in the opposite direction, they would cross paths by the end of the third day.

These were ALL pretty big ifs. Erik could have hiked west. He may have been too hurt to even make it to the big river. He could be dead already. Peter knew it was all a gamble but he was confident he had made the best decision that he could based on the information he had.

The night was falling and it was time to set up

camp. Peter's men set up their tents, made a fire and started prepping for a small meal. Commander Emmerick had landed safely and set up a base camp a few thousand feet below the wreckage. He had split his mixed team of CER and RCMP men into two teams and had made a grid map of one hundred square miles. The grid covered the entire south side of the mountain, clear down the valley all the way to the South Nahanni. The two teams would go over every section of the grid with a fine-tooth comb. Peter was happy with both the plan and their progress.

The Fort Laird RCMP men were approaching the crash site from the west, searching one hundred yards out from the river's edge, the same as Peter's team. The Fort Laird team was hiking through much rougher and swampy terrain but still should intersect with Emmerick's team by the end of the second day.

That left Peter's team. If they found nothing by the end of the fourth night it was over. It would be time to pack up and close the case for good. Peter was happy with the time his team was making and he knew they would cover their ground in four days.

The plan was in place and working well, now it was all up to Erik Keller to hold up his end of the deal.

# Chapter 37

Erik had been up and awake far before the sun broke over the horizon. The looming specter of the wolves had kept him on the ragged edge, unable to rest. His fever remained and was weakening him by the minute. He was mindful to keeping drinking and attempt to extinguish the fever, but he was losing the battle. Again, he tried to eat some of the smoked caribou but could not force himself to eat more than a few bites.

He was weak and in his mind he knew he would not be able to travel much longer. Perhaps tonight he would find a clearing and begin to make a giant fire in hopes of using it as some sort of signal. He could make a decent camp out of rocks to keep as safe as possible from the predators that seemed intent on stalking him.

Yes, Erik thought, this has to be the plan.

Push as far as I can tonight and set up for a rescue that may never come. It wasn't really a choice, he was spent. Erik packed his to bags on their frame, hoisted it onto his back, and started walking.

Travel became more tiring with every step and Erik found himself stopping very often to rest. He was along the river bank and other than the rock and boulder hopping, it was relatively level ground. The temperature wasn't terribly cold, not that Erik would have noticed with his fever.

After pushing himself as long as possible, Erik decided to rest out of the sun, slightly away from the river. It was midday and he needed to gear up for one final push. He stretched out on a mossy area at the base of a large spruce tree and attempted to take a quick nap. He was not quite out when an unfamiliar noise made him sit upright.

Unsure what it was, Erik pulled his gun from its holster and held incredibly still. What was that noise? It almost sounded like human laughter? The river!! The sounds were coming from the river!!

Erik leaped to his feet and moved as fast as his battered body could move. He burst through the brush and reached the river bank just as it went by.

It was a raft, bright and orange, with several people on it. Adventurers, running the rapids and having the time of their lives as they flew on down the South Nahanni. Erik stood there and watched as the raft floated out of sight. He hadn't seen or spoken to another human in several days and the sight of these happy people left him in a state of shock.

He almost didn't see the second raft approaching.

This time Erik snapped out of it. He jumped up and down and waved his arms and began screaming as loud as he ever had in his life.

"HEEYYY!! HERE! I'M OVER HERE!! LOOK OVER HERE!!!"

Just as quickly as the first raft came and went, so did the second. The Nahanni was over one hundred yards wide and very loud and the people on that raft weren't looking for plane crash survivors. They could not have heard him.

Maybe, at the very least, someone saw him, Erik hoped. He broke a large branch from a pine tree. If another raft came by he would wave it, maybe make it easier to be spotted. He sat on the bank and waited. He waited for half an hour.

No more rafts came by.

Erik sat in silence and decided what to make of the situation. It was very late in the season for rafters, from what he had read. But if this group was out there it could be possible to see others. The more people there were in the Nahanni National Park Reserve, the better his chance of being spotted. If there were helicopters dropping these people off then there was a good chance they could spot a large fire.

Yes, tonight's fire would be the thing that saves him. Erik Keller picked up his pack and moved on down the bank to look for a suitable clearing.

# Chapter 38

Peter awoke to his phone alarm, warm in his sleeping bag with Winnie snoring next to him. It was daybreak and as he exited his tent he was pleased to see the CER men were already up and packing, ready to attack the day.

"Timmons, make sure you men get something to eat and fill those canteens. We are going to cover a lot of ground today."

"Yes, sir. Way ahead of you sir."

Emmerick may be an asshole and his team over-promoted, but the men accompanying Peter were working hard and starting to grow on him. He would make sure to mention it when he wrote his final report on the case. These men shouldn't be discounted because of poor leadership, in Peter's opinion.

Before the sun was fully over the ridge, Peter and his team were on their feet and searching the river bank and surrounding areas. The sky was slightly greyer than the previous day and Peter made a mental note to have Marchont give him a full weather report the next time they spoke.

The team stayed quiet as they searched, they were making good time and Peter was hopeful that they could push to the twenty-mile mark today. Even in the best case scenario, he was doubtful Erik Keller could have made it this far downriver so soon, but the team was taking no chances and checked the area thoroughly.

Soon it was midday and Peter's team stopped to have lunch and rest for thirty minutes. All of the men sat along a car-sized boulder and drank water from the clean Nahanni. They fueled up on energy bars, almonds, and apples. Fast, light, and easy meals were necessary for this kind of travel. Peter even made a little small talk with the other men before radioing his coordinates to Marchont.

"You're making good time Sgt." Marchont informed him. "You are on pace for about eighteen miles by sundown. Sir, it looks like heavy rains coming in after dark. One more thing

Sir, good news. Commander Emmerick's team found definite signs of boot tracks coming down the ridge from the wreck. They also found what they think is a very simple shelter made of fir branches at around five thousand feet. Sir, it looks as if Mr. Keller survived at least one night after the crash."

"Does Lauren know this?" asked Peter.

"No sir, she went to Anita's for lunch. Said the stress of waiting was making her crazy. Should I tell her, Sir?"

Peter thought about it for a moment.

"Tell her we found definite signs that he walked away from the wreckage......hold off on telling her about the campsite. I don't want to give her false hope until we know more. If Keller stayed in that shelter it would have been several days ago. That is a long time."

"Yes, Sir. Copy that."

"Marchont, in the meantime instruct Commander Emmerick to put two of our men on the tracks leading from that shelter. Maybe they can stay on his path."

"Will do, Sir. Oh, one more thing, there is somebody else here who wants to say 'Hello'."

Peter waited for a minute until he heard the friendly voice come out of his two-way.

"Hey, Peter, Ron Jenkins here. Don't worry, you're still in charge, I'm just checking in a couple of times a day."

Peter laughed out loud, "We are glad to have you there Lt."

"Not Lieutenant Pete, not anymore. I faxed my papers in last night. Beat Emmerick to the punch. I am officially retired."

"Congrats, Ron. First beer is on me when we get back. Over and out."

Peter smiled, he knew it was an open frequency and Emmerick had most likely been listening. He wouldn't get a chance to ruin Ron. He left on his own accord.

"Saddle up, boys."

Peter had a little pep in his step as the team headed off down the river bank.

# Chapter 39

Fever was now overwhelming Erik's body. He needed to find a clearing, set up camp and make that fire soon. His entire body ached, his broken left hand and wrist hurting more than it had at any time during the trip. He was soaked with sweat right through his jeans, undershirt and flannel shirt.

The pack he carried felt heavier than ever and his back ached, but he continued on. Eventually, Erik found himself at the foot of another ridge, a smaller ridge, but it was still an obstacle. He sat by the river and drank some water.

He had to fight this infection the best he could and right now his only medicine was to stay hydrated. Remembering the whiskey Erik pulled the bottle from his pack. He took off the cap, pulled up his right pant leg and poured whiskey directly on to the old wound. His leg looked and smelled terrible and it was so infected and swollen that he didn't even feel the sting of pain that usually came when he applied the whiskey.

He had no idea if it would even help but he was at the end of his rope and had no other resources. There were no more than a couple of ounces left in the bottle when he capped it and returned it to its place in the backpack. There were no more clean socks to redress the wound with and it probably wouldn't make a difference at this point anyway.

Erik had only one goal now, to climb this ridge, find a clearing, and set up what would be his final campsite. Quite possibly the last campsite he would EVER prepare. Maybe even his final resting spot. Erik knew things were looking grim.

None the less, he hoisted that heavy pack across his shoulders one last time and started climbing. The incline should have been simple to negotiate, even for an injured man, but Erik was in terrible condition. Every step was a challenge and he stopped every few steps to catch his breath.

His legs felt heavy and he continually rubbed his eyes, which he had trouble keeping focused.

The incline was only a couple hundred feet but it took Erik well over an hour to reach the summit. When he did, he was thrilled with what he saw. On the other side of the ridge was a small patch of forest and just past that, on the edge of the river, was a large clearing.

"Perfect," Erik said aloud.

The clearing was only an acre or two but it was open, next to the river and could easily be seen from the air. All that was left was to get off this ridge, make shelter, start a huge fire and wait. Erik felt confident that if he could get past those barriers he could make it a couple of more days.

Darkness was approaching as he started off down the ridge. Slowly he placed his feet against the rocks and lowered himself down, sliding on his rear. It was a method he repeated many times since the crash. It was time-consuming and awkward, especially with the heavy pack, but it was the only way. Erik continued on this way without stopping for over an hour. He was near to the bottom when it happened.

He placed his right foot against a rock and

stood to get his balance when suddenly the rock became dislodged. Erik lurched forward, the weight of his pack causing momentum, and began tumbling down the ridge. He fought, to no avail, to gain a grip with his hands and feet as he fell. Several times he hurtled head over heels until he found his body sliding feet forward into a pile of stones at the bottom of the hill. He braced himself for an impact he couldn't avoid.

His right foot slid in between two rocks, his body rolling to the left.

CRACK!!!

He screamed in pain and right away Erik knew what the sickening sound was. He lay on his stomach, fresh blood on his elbows and forehead. He had broken his right ankle, there was no doubt. For a few minutes, he laid there, pain shooting from the ankle.

Slowly he began to crawl. Soon he saw his pack in front of him. He tried to drag it along with him. He had to try for the river. His head felt heavy and he was having trouble seeing.

Erik Keller was able to pull himself up against a large boulder where, as darkness enveloped him, he lost consciousness.

# Chapter 40

Peter and his team had a very good day. There were no signs of their missing man, but he didn't really expect any until tomorrow at the earliest anyway. They were well on their way to hitting their eighteen-mile goal for the day.

The biggest surprise of the day was two rafts filled with outdoor adventurers passing by. They were braving the rapids and enjoying themselves. Peter couldn't help but think it was getting a little late in the year for them to be out. The group did not even notice Peter's team as they zipped on by.

Winnie was having the time of her life. She thrived in these situations and was always happiest on the trail. She had a habit of traveling well ahead of the team, an advance scout so to speak. If she found something, whether it was a scent or a tangible item, she would bark to alert Peter of her position. During past searches, on more than one occasion, she came face to face with a bear or two. Winnie always won these confrontations, the much larger predators scampering off into the forest.

It was nearing the end of the day and the terrain had become much rockier with more underbrush blocking access to the river bank. Peter hated losing sight of the water, but they couldn't walk through the tangled mess, neither could their survivor.

The team came upon an elevated rocky ledge that sat about twenty feet above the river and decided to make camp for the night. Peter radioed his final coordinates to Marchont at the command center and was happy to find out they had covered nineteen miles that day. The bad news was that another massive canyon was straight ahead and they would have a hard time coming anywhere near that distance tomorrow.

To make matters worse, Marchont informed him that a major storm system would be over them for the next day and a half and they would be dealing with steady rains and wind.

"Marchont, is Mrs. Keller there?"

"I'm right here Peter", her voice coming over the transmitter.

"Nothing yet, I am sorry to say. The next two days will be critical, I am hoping to find something by then."

"You were very clear about your goal of four days. I can't ask for anything more."

Peter hated to constantly be the bearer of bad news. He had grown extremely fond of Lauren Keller in the short time he had known her. She had pushed his boundaries and made him re-think some of his plans for the future. Once again he was telling her that he had nothing to report, and once again she was understanding and thankful.

"Peter," Lauren continued," I've made a decision. I'm leaving at the end of the fourth day. I'll be gone by the time you all return from the park. My boys have been without me for long enough. Ron helped me with the flights. I'm hopeful for the next two days, but I have to be realistic too. The minute your team meets with the others, if you have found nothing, I will be out of here."

Peter took a moment before he responded.

"I understand, Ma'am, family first. I am still hoping for a miracle, as I know you are. It has been my pleasure to know you. Over and out."

"Good night and good luck, Peter."

For the longest time, Peter sat on the ledge, his feet dangling over the edge. The sheer power of the water roaring below him as he was lost in thought. He hated unresolved cases. The need for finality was a driving force behind him and always had been. Now, he had forty-eight hours to get some kind of resolution. The terrain was getting worse, as was the weather, and little did he know the worst was yet to come.

It was Timmons who broke the news.

"Sir, I've just received orders from Commander Emmerick. We are to give him coordinates for an extraction tomorrow at seven AM. We are being pulled from the search, sir."

"What?!?! We are only halfway to our objective. Whose call is this?"

"Commander Emmerick didn't say sir."

Peter was furious; Emmerick had promised him that his team would stay engaged for the duration of the operation. He contacted Marchont

252

and demanded to be put through to the Commander. After a few minutes, the connection was made.

"Emmerick, what the hell is going on here?"

"We have been given orders from the top, Sgt. There are some dignitaries from Asia flying into Edmonton tomorrow night and the Prime Minister wants my team on the tarmac in dress uniform to greet them."

"So you are leaving a search so they can parade you around and show you off to a bunch of foreign politicians??"

For the first time since they had met Peter thought he heard some humility and sincerity in Emmerick's voice.

"Sgt. McEwan, I am sorry. If it was my call my boys would be staying here on the ground. This kind of search and rescue is invaluable for my men; they are learning things that they can't train for otherwise. Unfortunately, we are at the beck and call of our government. They fund us, I can't say no. My men will be gathered up and flown out of here in the morning. I hope you find your man, Peter. Good Luck."

Peter stood there with his radio in his hand.

What could he do but deal with it? This entire operation had been thrown curveballs from the start. He didn't expect to have support from the CER in the first place, but after Emmerick pledged his men it made Peter change his plans. Now he would have to change them again.

"Marchont, did you hear all of that?"

"Unfortunately, I did, Sir," the young Officer replied.

"Change of plans. When the Fort Laird team intersects with the mountain team I have new orders. Half of the Fort Laird team will stay on the mountain with our men and continue the grid search. The other half will keep pushing east toward me. We should meet by the end of day four."

"What about you, Sir?"

"Winnie and I will continue on alone. I'll stay to the river bank. I will contact you at sunrise. Over and out."

Peter was solemn as he pitched his tent. It was dark now and the CER men kept their distance from him, they knew he was disappointed. He fed Winnie, ate an apple and crawled into his tent. Two more days and it would be back to life as usual.

Winnie curled up against Peter just as the first raindrops hit the roof of their little tent.

# Chapter 41

When Erik came to he was unsure of where he was. It was raining very heavy and he was cold and very confused. His body was shaking violently and his right ankle was throbbing. With much pain and effort, he sat up against the large boulder where he had passed out earlier.

Then he remembered, he remembered everything, the crash, the journey, and the fall that broke his ankle. Now here he was, fully exposed to the freezing rain, infection running through his body. Hope was lost and he couldn't possibly survive the night, could he? He could see nothing, not that it mattered, his vision had been fuzzy and failing him even before the fall.

Blindly reaching around, he found his pack. It was the trusty pack that he had fashioned from branches and had secured his two backpacks and sleeping bag to. The pack that had been his enemy during those long climbs, the pack that had been his friend when he needed supplies from it.

He unzipped one of the backpacks, found a raincoat and put it on. Unrolling and unzipping the old torn sleeping bag, he pulled it over his body. It reminded him of making a blanket fort when he was a child. He was already cold and wet, but maybe he could hope to keep some of his body heat trapped under the coat and bag.

Erik Keller was having no illusions and did not expect to survive until morning.

That is how he spent the rest of the night, weaving in and out of consciousness, sitting upright against a rock. He dreamed fever dreams when he was out. He dreamed he was at Disney World with Lauren and the boys. He dreamed about fishing with John on the banks of Sterling Creek in their little hometown. He dreamed of Christmas morning when the boys were little, a hot cup of coffee in his hand, joy in his heart.

At times he almost thought the dreams were real. Then the cold and the rain and the pain would bring him back to his bleak reality. It went on this way all night.

Erik awoke again, peeking his head out from the soaking wet sleeping bag he realized that it was day time. It was still raining, not quite as heavy, but now Erik could see his surroundings. There was a tree line fifty yards away and beyond that, he could hear the river.

Erik knew that he needed to reach the river, his last hope of survival lay on its banks. Erik was so weak he could barely sit upright, but he knew he had to try to get there.

Reaching into his bag he found the last of his paracord. With great trouble, trying to use his broken left hand, he attempted to tie his sleeping bag to his belt. Erik's motor skills were failing him and between that and his wavering vision, it took a great deal of time to tie the required knots.

Finally, he secured the bag to himself. He took his remaining supplies, including his gun, and buried them deep within the zipped up bag. He knew he couldn't walk and would have to crawl. With the sleeping bag tied to his belt, he would pull his broken body to the water.

He screamed aloud as he rolled from a sitting position to his belly. Using his good right arm he reached out and attempted to pull his body along the ground. Seething pain shot up his fractured right leg as it dragged over the stones.

*I can't do it...I can't make it!!*

Tears rolled down his cheeks and Erik could taste their saltiness. He had willed his broken and battered body along every inch of this journey and now he needed just a little more. Erik let out a guttural scream and reached out again. He pulled himself a few inches further, and again pain surged through his body.

He repeated this process several times over the course of the next hours, willing himself when he had nothing left to give. Fifty yards later, just as he reached the trees, he once again passed out from the pain and fell back into his dreams.

# Chapter 42

When Peter unzipped the door of his tent to let Winnie out to relieve herself it was still raining heavily. The CER men were in full rain gear, complete with their damned CER logo, and were breaking down their tents. Peter set himself to doing the same as Winnie gave him an annoyed look. She was willing to work in the rain, but she didn't have to like it. Peter was just putting his pack on his back when he was approached by Timmons.

"Sir, we are awfully sorry to have to leave sir. We are heading three hundred yards back to a clearing to await our pick up. Good luck, Sir."

Timmons stuck out his hand and Peter shook it firmly.

"You boys are just following orders. That's what you're supposed to do. You guys did well out here, maybe we will work together again someday."

"I hope so, Sir. Again, good luck and stay safe."

Timmons and his two fellow team members turned back and soon disappeared into the wilderness.

"C'mon, Win. Let's keep moving before we freeze to death."

They started the long climb alone up the canyon wall. The conditions were dangerous, many of the rocks were covered with several varieties of moss and lichen and the rain made everything slippery. Winnie seemed unbothered by the terrain as she hopped from boulder to boulder like a mountain lion. Many times she looked back at Peter, irritated by his pace which was much slower and more deliberate.

By midday, the rain was letting up and Peter and Winnie were at the apex of the ridge. The river looked small and winding from their height and Peter guessed they were near one thousand feet up. He fed Winnie some jerky and gave her a few drinks from his canteen before having a long pull from it himself. It was time to give Marchont a progress report.

"McEwan to base. Come in base."

"Base on Sgt. Are you well?"

"Everything is fine here. Did the CER get all of their men picked up safely?"

"They did, Sir. They are on their way to Edmonton as we speak. Good news, the Fort Laird group met with our guys south of the wreck first thing this morning. They split up as you ordered and are making incredible time in your direction. If you both move at your current pace you should meet up by noon tomorrow."

"Very Good. Is Mrs. Keller there?"

"No, Sir. Lt, err... Mr. Jenkins took her to lunch and is helping her with travel arrangements."

"O.K., I'll be in touch with my coordinates during the day. Over and out."

Peter reached down and scratched Winnie behind the ears.

"Well girl, tomorrow might be the last day you and I ever do this together. I'm just about done. You?"

Winnie gave him a look of indifference as she

impatiently waited to get back on the move. Peter let out a hearty laugh and the two of them headed down off the ridge.

The trip down was relatively uneventful and by four PM they were back on flat ground and making good time along the river. Peter was lost in thought, running through his options and Winnie was forging ahead, ever vigilant. Peter was surprised during his last check-in when Marchont informed him they had put twelve miles behind them.

As he had done from the start Peter scanned left and right as he hiked, looking for anything that appeared out of place. Clothing, an old campfire, a broken branch, any of these could be a sign that Erik Keller had been through the area.

Alas, he had seen nothing in his travels that gave him any indication Erik had been through here. Winnie's nose would have picked up on anything of note far before Peter would see it anyway. Peter was surprised that the grid search had not uncovered Erik's body. Last night was the final straw, the cold and rain would have been impossible for an injured, starving man to endure.

It was getting dark now. Peter and Winnie set

up their tent, started a small fire and ate. The sky had cleared and the stars were brilliant in the sky. A lot of soul searching went on that night.

After checking in one last time with headquarters, he crawled into his tent with Winnie. Peter climbed inside of his bag and went to sleep, discouraged.

# Chapter 43

Erik Keller regained consciousness about an hour before dark. Again, he had no clue where he was and it took some time to get acclimated to his surroundings. He remembered trying to reach the tree line and apparently he has succeeded because he was lying under an enormous spruce.

He attempted to sit upright but there was a weight holding him back, only then did he look down and remember having tied the sleeping bag to himself. By using his right hand to pull the bag even with his body he was able to sit upright against the tree.

The forest was quiet and he could hear the river rushing along just beyond the trees. It had been his goal but he wouldn't be reaching it tonight. Erik was starting to hallucinate and he thought he saw a helicopter fly above. He was having trouble trusting himself and knew his body was in the final stages of shutting down.

Erik was going nowhere but he still had sense enough to know he had to try and make it through the night. The giant spruce tree had roots protruding from the ground that was nearly two feet above ground level. Erik had managed to pull his broken body in between two of these roots and was nestled in a sort of little cave. Like the previous night, he pulled the damp sleeping bag over himself.

In moments of clarity, he wondered how in the hell he was still alive. It must have been nearly two weeks since his crash, and his injuries were plenty. He had suffered from blood loss, broken bones, and the elements. All he had eaten were a few fish and that wonderful two days that he gorged on caribou meat. The jerky he had spent all that precious time making had finally turned bad and with his fever the past few days he hadn't eaten much.

Erik sat in the dark, wavering in and out of fever dreams. He was severely dehydrated now, his kidneys most likely shutting down. He was becoming numb to the pain and the end couldn't be far off.

It was because of his deteriorated state that he did not see the first wolf.

Erik smelled the creature before he saw it. It reminded him of the smell of a wet deer in the rain after a hunt. There was a flash not five feet to his right. Something was tugging at the end of the sleeping bag, attempting to get into the backpack.

It was suddenly clear to Erik that it was a wolf. With what might have been his last drop of adrenaline he let out a maniacal scream.

"AHHHHHHHHH!!!!!"

The animal was startled and retreated several yards back. Erik pulled the backpack close to him, remembering his gun was inside. He dug through the pack and finding his weapon, pulled the Glock from its holster and pointed it with his right hand. By now two more wolves had joined the first and they paced back and forth in front of Erik.

Was this really happening? Was he hallucinating? How many bullets did he have left? He tried to clear his foggy mind and recall. Five? As best he could remember there were five shots left in that gun. In any case, he wasn't about to remove the clip and start counting them.

Erik's scream did not deter the beasts and they brazenly came closer, growling and nipping at the other backpack. *It must be the jerky they smell*, thought Erik. It was either that or his rotting leg.

Erik raised the pistol above his head and pulled the trigger, a single round flying off into the night. It was his hope that the wolves would be scared off, and they did retreat nearly out of his sight. But after a few minutes, they once again returned, determined to get a meal for their trouble.

The stars and moonlit the sky well that night and Erik could see a decent distance out from his tree. The wolves began to gather again, this time joined by others. As they paced and circled Erik tried to keep track of them but he could not ascertain how many there were. Once again they were only a few feet away, and once again he fired his weapon into the night sky.

Again the wolves retreated, but this time not nearly as far. They were getting braver and the sound of the gun was not frightening them as Erik hoped it would. The next time the group grew close Erik put his sights square on the largest wolf that he could clearly see. The animal was not ten feet away when he shot his gun.

CRACKKKK!!!!!

First, the sound of the shot rang out, and then the yelp of an injured animal followed. Erik had hit his target and he could hear a great commotion in the brush as the wolf screamed in pain and thrashed on the ground. The reaction of the beast had caused the others to run off, but for how long?

For a few moments, Erik held perfectly still, holding his breath and trying to focus his vision. At first, there was nothing, but then he saw movement. One lone wolf hovered at the edge of the light, just within Erik's sight. Without thinking he lifted his gun and fired, again striking his intended target. This wolf carried on much more than the first, wailing and shrieking for several minutes. Erik could hear the remaining wolves running off into the woods. They were gone, for now. Erik struggled to remember how many bullets were left, but it was much too dark to check.

Several minutes passed before Erik's fever won out against his will to stay awake. He passed out, the last of his energy used up. His gun fell from his hand onto the ground before him as he entered into the dream world once more.

# Chapter 44

When the sun rose on the fourth and final day of the ground search it found Sgt. Peter McEwan and his rescue dog Winnie ready to go. They had risen early, broke down camp and eaten. Peter, if not Winnie, was ready to return home to his shower and warm woodstove. He and Winnie would give it their best on this final day, but part of Peter was glad he wouldn't have to face Lauren one last time, in failure without a body for her to take back to the states.

He had given Marchont specific instructions to relay to the mountain/wreck site team. They were to complete a final grid search and be ready for evacuation by four PM. According to Marchont, the Ft. Laird RCMP team would meet him coming from the west by midday. The entire group would find or make, a clearing for their evacuation. A debriefing would take place at the Watson Lake RCMP detachment where a press release would be sent out, final reports written and all of the men returned to their normal details.

This meant conservation work, criminal investigation and regular road patrols for most of the men. It would not for Peter. His mind was at peace, this would be his last time in the field. With Ron Jenkins retired it would mean new leadership in Watson Lake. Sgt. McEwan had been through several regime changes in his career and he would not be sticking around for another. His minimum retirement service time of twenty-five years would be up in mid-October and he, like Ron before him, would be filing his papers soon.

Before long Peter and Winnie were hiking again. The sun was bringing warmth and even though the regular high temperature was only around forty degrees that would be enough to break a sweat hiking in this rough country. They stuck to the river bank, Winnie patrolling several hundred yards ahead per usual. Peter kept a sharp eye out for any irregularities.

The Nahanni was particularly beautiful on this sunny September day. The light glistened off of the breaking water as the ancient river flowed over centuries-old rock. Many of the hardwood trees had lost their leaves, but the evergreens that made up the majority of the forest had kept their brilliant greens. Several hawks circled, hunting for a meal, and occasionally a trout leaped from the water.

Peter wondered how badly he would miss it all.

Returning to the southern border area of his beloved Canada meant less time spent in the remote country he loved. There would always be visits to old friends and co-workers and such. It was the everyday life in the populated areas that Peter worried about. Could he adapt? It was thoughts like these that pushed him through that final morning's work.

There was another thing that tugged at his mind.

He had been awakened last night by what he could have sworn were gunshots. There was no hunting in the Nahanni and it was night. The possibility that the shots came from poachers was very real, but all of the RCMP officers were armed too. The gunshots could have simply been one of his own men scaring off a troublesome bear. Either way, he would make sure to include it in his report.

Checking his watch Peter saw that the time was half-past ten in the AM. He stopped at the riverbank, bent down and filled his canteen with cold water. He was just finishing a long pull from it when he heard a commotion in the distance.

It was Winnie. She was barking loudly, something she rarely did. It would not be the first time Winnie tried picking a fight with a larger opponent. This time there was a different tone to her barking as if she were in trouble or needed Peter urgently.

Peter capped his canteen and broke off into a run towards the sound of his faithful girl.

# Chapter 45

Darkness.

Erik Keller was in total darkness, unsure if he was alive or dead. The pain that had encompassed his entire body for the past two weeks was not present. There was only thirst. An awful thirst, like he had not had a drink in forever. Erik sat still for the longest time.

Hearing the breeze and the sound of birds, he finally decided to move. Lifting his right arm slightly caused his sleeping bag to fall from around his head and shoulders and suddenly Erik was assaulted with bright light. He began to make out the shapes of the trees and boulders before him.

He was alive.

Somehow, against all probability, he had

made it through another cold night in the Nahanni. His head was impossibly foggy, his vision blurred and failing him, but he was most definitely alive. Erik was in a state he had never experienced before. His thoughts were mostly clear, but his body and eyes felt as if they belonged to an intoxicated man. His body wasn't obeying his commands and every act or movement seemed to require total focus.

He was losing motor skills and quickly. Blood loss, infection, and dehydration had left him near the brink of death. The fact that his pain levels were down worried Erik the most, even his crushed left wrist and hand were only slightly numb.

Thirst was the most important thing to him at the moment, he needed to drink. His head was clear enough to remember that the river was just beyond the trees, and now Erik would go to that river. He may very well die before he reached the water's edge but death did not even worry him anymore. Unsure why he was even still alive, he was determined to drink.

With great effort, Erik rolled to his side, and then to his stomach. Reaching out with his right arm he dug his right elbow into the stone and dirt. He pulled his body with his good arm and pushed with his toes on his left foot. Standing was not an option as he did not have the strength or balance to accomplish such a feat. Slowly he repeated the process.

The pain began to return as Erik crawled and he welcomed it like an old friend. Pain meant he was still alive, and as long as he was he wouldn't quit. His shin and ankle began to throb, as did his ribs and his bad arm.

He could hear the river now and it only caused him to become hyper-focused. The thought of the cold, clear Nahanni river water touching his lips was like a fire beneath him, driving him forward. Unlike the day before he would not stop to rest, there was only forward.

The sounds of the river were distinct now, there was no doubt he was close. He could not yet see it, but he could hear it and even smell it. With his right hand Erik struggled to untie the sleeping bag and back pack that were tied to his body. They were slowing him down and he needed to reach his destination.

There was no way for him to tell time, to

know how long he had been crawling. He only knew that the sun was bright and the river near. His jeans had long ago become tattered and ripped and he could feel the cool ground against his thighs and stomach as he crawled.

There it was!!!!

Impossibly, brilliantly blue. It was mere yards away.

Erik's vision became clearer and he could make out the boulders protruding from the river. He could see the water splashing against the shore. Cold, wet relief was just out of his grasp. Replenishment awaited, soon he could drink, rest, re-focus, plan.

Maybe even live another day.

Just as Erik was ready to lower his face into the water a flashing object caught his attention. Something was running down the bank towards him, an animal.

The Wolves!!!

Erik reached down for his gun. It was not there, he had left it back at the tree.

The wolf was bearing down on him quickly and he knew this was the end. Erik tensed up his body and waited for the impact. He readied himself for the gnashing of teeth and the sweet embrace of death. He only hoped it would be quick.

"I'm sorry, Lauren," he whispered, just as the wolf pounced.

And like that it happened.

He could feel the weight of the animal on his chest. But something was wrong. He was not being bitten.....he was being licked. The animal licked his face and neck and began to bark.

The friendly wolf barked louder and louder and Erik lay perfectly still, confused but alive.

# Chapter 46

Peter's heart was beating hard in his chest, partially due to the fact he was hustling over rocky, uneven territory. But mostly he was afraid Winnie was in some sort of danger. He moved as fast as he safely could, he did not want to fall and injure himself.

Winnie continued to bark repeatedly and Peter realized he was less than fifty yards away from her. He unsnapped the holster, ready to draw his sidearm if necessary. There was a thick stand of brush that Peter had to push through, he became entangled for a minute, but broke free into a small clearing on a bend in the river. When he entered the clearing he couldn't believe what he was seeing.

There, on the embankment, was Winnie and she was happily licking a disheveled looking man who was lying feet from the water. For a moment Peter was speechless, the man seemed to be making eye contact with him, but didn't seem to really trust his eyes.

"Are you Erik Keller?" Peter asked.

The man was dirty, covered in dried blood and his face was pale. His clothing was ripped and he was wearing only one boot. He slowly propped himself up on one elbow.

"Yeah, I'm Erik. Is this real.......are you really here?"

Peter felt a wave of relief wash over him and he let out a hearty laugh.

"Your damn right I'm real my friend, and I'm here to take you home!"

Peter slid down the bank and grabbed Erik under the arms, pulling him up onto the flat ground. Without a word he opened his canteen and handed it to Erik. When Erik tried lift it to his mouth his hand shook violently and only then did Peter understand how weak and spent the man was.

"Hang on partner; I'll hold it for you."

Peter propped Erik up and poured the water slowly into his mouth. Erik drank slowly but repeatedly and finished the entire canteen.

"More. Can I get more?"

Peter scurried to the river and got a refill. Soon he was helping Erik to drink again.

"Listen to me Erik, I know you're weak and things might seem a little foggy, but I need you to keep talking to me, O.K."

The water had brought Erik around a bit and his head was a little clearer.

"O.K. I'm O.K. Who are you?"

"I am Sergeant Peter McEwan of the Royal Canadian Mounted Police. I've been looking for you for nearly two weeks."

"You have....?"

"Sorry buddy, the Nahanni's a big park. Now listen, here's what we're going to do. I am going to treat you best I can here and then we are going to radio in a chopper and get you the hell out of here. Sound good?"

If Erik hadn't been so dehydrated he would have cried; still there was a lot of emotion in his voice when he replied.

"Yes Sgt. I'm ready. I want to go home."

"Call me Peter. Erik, can you tell me about your injuries?"

"My right hand and wrist....they're broken. Crushed , I think. I have a bad cut on my right shin. It's infected. I think it's in my bloodstream. I broke my ankle two nights ago......I think it was two nights ago..... that's why I have been stuck in this spot."

"Alright, let me take a look," Peter said.

He looked at the hand and wrist first. The skin was green and black from swelling and it was obvious there were several fractures. Peter then tore away what remained of the jeans around Erik's infected leg, exposing his injury. What he saw was bad, the leg was discolored and smelled like rotting flesh. Erik was right, the infection was most definitely in his blood and this made the situation more urgent.

Using some dry branches he found on the ground, and some paracord from his pack, Peter devised a splint for the broken ankle. He warned Erik that it would hurt right before he tightened all of the paracord. To his credit Erik did not scream out, although he winced and was in obvious discomfort. It was a rough piece of work, but it only had to suffice until they reached the clearing.

Peter broke out his first aid kit and went to work on Erik's other wounds. He handed Erik a candy bar before he started.

"Here, we have to get some calories in you fast. Have you eaten?"

"Three fish. And some caribou.....but most of it went bad."

"Caribou. How?"

"I shot it. I had my gun with me. It's back in the woods with my pack."

"No kidding?? Hey Erik, did you fire your gun last night?"

"Yes, at some wolves. I thought your dog was a wolf when she found me."

"Haha. No, she only thinks she's a wolf. Anyway, she and your wife have become fast friends."

"My wife....?"

"Yes, Mr. Keller. She's here, in Watson Lake. She was here within three days of your crash. She's been staying at our station and making sure everyone stays on point. You are a lucky man, Erik. Lauren was bound and determined to make sure we found you."

Erik had trouble believing what he was

hearing. Lauren was here, in the Territories? She had been only a few miles away from Erik for the entirety of this whole ordeal?

"Is there a way I can speak to her?"

"Yes. Let me get you treated first and then we will call in an evacuation."

Peter had wrapped Erik's hand and wrist in gauze and fashioned a sling out of a tee-shirt. He helped Erik to sit up against a tree and placed the sling around his neck. Next, he used alcohol wipes to clean Erik's leg wound before wrapping it in the remaining gauze. He then gave Erik four ibuprofen.

"Swallow these. It's not going to help much but it's better than nothing. Now we have two choices, there is a clearing a quarter of a mile back and it's big enough for a rescue chopper. I can drag you there or I can try and help you to walk."

"I'm feeling a little better. If I throw my arm over your shoulder and keep the weight off my ankle I think I can walk."

"O.K. Let's call that chopper. Then we can radio your wife."

Erik was overwhelmed with emotion. What would he say? The thought of Lauren and the boys had kept him alive in the Nahanni for almost two weeks but only now did he realize he never really did expect to survive. Now he was about to speak with his wife, for real.

"This is Sgt. McEwan to base, Marchont do you read me?"

Mere seconds later, the radio crackled to life.

"Base on, Sgt."

"Marchont, is Lauren still there?"

"Yes. She just came to say goodbye and was about to leave, Sir. I'll put her on."

Lauren spoke softly and sadly. It was the voice of a defeated woman.

"Peter, I'm sorry to leave without saying goodbye to you. It's just so....."

Peter interrupted her.

"Well hold on one minute, Mrs. Keller. I have someone here who wants to speak to you."

"What??"

Peter had a huge grin on his face as he handed the radio to Erik. Erik nervously took the radio into his hand, took a deep breath and keyed the mic.

"Hey, Honey. Sorry, I'm late. Did you miss me?"

"Erik?!?? Oh my, God!! Is it really you???"

Her heart was beating rapidly in her chest and tears instantly began to stream down her face. She became light-headed and lost her balance, but Marchont placed both arms around her shoulders to steady her.

"I'm O.K. How are the boys? Are they alright?"

"Oh, Erik!! They are going to be so happy to see you. I can't believe it. How? Are you hurt? How did you make it?"

"I'll tell you everything when I see you. I love you, baby."

"I love you so much. I'll be waiting."

Peter, still grinning, took control of the radio once more.

"Lauren, put Marchont back on."

"Peter, thank you so much. Thank you, Thank you.....here, here he is."

Marchont's voice broke over the airwaves.

"I can't believe it Sarge, this is insane. What do you need?"

"Call in an evac for me, I'll send my coordinates in roughly one hour. Have the boys on the mountain picked up early. Tell Fort Laird to hurry and maybe they can ride with us, if not we'll send the chopper back for them. I need an ambulance fueled up and ready to go to Whitehorse. Make sure they have antibiotics and saline. Mr. Keller is dehydrated, has multiple fractures and a serious blood infection, we have to treat it ASAP. We are making for a clearing now, get those birds in the air."

"Yes, Sir."

Peter put the radio back on his belt and looked at Erik.

"You ready to go, my friend?"

"My backpack," said Erik, "It's back there a couple of hundred feet. There is something in it I need."

# Chapter 47

The midday sun was high in the sky and Erik marveled at it, now able to once again take in the Nahanni's wonder and beauty. Peter had retrieved his backpack and was kind enough to strap it to his own as he helped Erik along a few steps at a time. The process was slow and many times Erik banged his newly broken ankle and winced in pain.

"I have to take a break, Peter," Erik said, as he sat on a large rock.

"No problem, buddy. We are just a few hundred yards from the clearing for evacuation. The chopper is en route, just waiting on our final coordinates. It should be no more than sixty minutes. How are you feeling?"

"The candy bar and nuts you gave me are working. I can feel my energy coming back. Peter, did your team find the crash site? My friend,

John, did you find him?"

Once again Peter was the bearer of bad news. He took a deep breath and looked Erik in the eye.

"We only discovered the wreck four days ago, which in turn spurred the ground search. Before that, we had no starting point. Part of my team dropped in on the site. They found two bodies, one of which was John Woodsley. I'm sorry. I assure you; he died on impact and didn't suffer."

"Thanks. I knew in my heart he was gone. I'm still trying to figure out how I even survived the crash. None of it makes any sense."

Both men sat in silence for a moment and Winnie came close to Erik looking for a scratch behind her ear. He was happy to oblige.

"What's your name, little wolf?"

"That would be 'Winnie', my partner for the last eight years. She is the only one who was willing to work with me."

Erik let out a little chuckle, perhaps the first time he had truly laughed in days.

"C'mon, let's reach the evacuation site. I can answer any more questions you have once we are there," Peter said.

He helped Erik to his feet and slowly, a step or

two at a time, they headed down the river for the clearing. Erik slung his right arm over Peter's shoulder and hopped on his left foot. Several times they stopped for Erik to catch his breath and regain his bearings. The two men continued to speak as they traveled.

Erik informed Peter of Gus's collapse and the ensuing scramble to control the plane. He told him of the first night, spent in the tail section, and of his decision to leave the crash site. He told him of fishing and the encounter with the bears. Before either man realized it nearly an hour passed and they had reached the evacuation site.

Peter radioed in the coordinates and was informed that the helicopter was less than fifteen minutes away. He opened a tin of tuna fish and made Erik down the whole thing, along with more water. Peter cleared some fallen branches and sticks from the landing site and prepared a flare to mark their spot when the time was ready. Both men then sat on the ground, their backs against a large boulder and waited as Winnie chased a butterfly in the clearing.

"Are you still feeling O.K.? More water?"

"No thanks, Peter. I'm feeling alright, I've

made it this far, I'm not going to die before I see my wife and get to a hospital."

"The chopper will be here in a few minutes. Erik, I'm awful sorry that your hunting trip turned into this nightmare. I promise you, Canada isn't always this bad," Peter said with a grin.

Erik took a deep breath and smiled.

"You know what? I came here looking for adventure and I sure as hell found it. The country, well.....even with everything I went through to get here, the beauty of the wilderness wasn't lost on me. This is truly an amazing place."

Peter looked around for a minute, taking it all in.

"Yes. Yes, it is."

Suddenly, Erik remembered something. A promise he made long ago to a friend that could no longer keep it. Maybe, he could honor John's spirit right here in the Nahanni, with a new friend. Erik reached over to his pack, which was still secured to Peters, and pulled out the bottle of Canadian Whisky.

Surprised, Peter let out a loud laugh.

"Where in the hell did you get that?"

Erik swirled the bottle around and the last few

ounces swished in the bottom of the bottle.

"It survived the crash with me. Peter, what do you say we have a toast and finish it right here and now?"

"Well, I am on duty, but what the hell. Open her up, my friend."

Erik removed the cap one last time and brought the bottle to his nose taking in a long whiff. He held the bottle high to the blue sky.

"To my friend, John Woodsley. We made it buddy."

Erik brought the bottle to his lips and took a drink, he could feel the warmth travel from his stomach and into his extremities. He handed the bottle over, the last swallow for Sgt. Peter McEwan.

"To John. May his memory live forever," Peter said as he tilted the bottle back and finished it off.

The two men sat in the clearing, against the rock in silence as a few hawks circled. The bird's silhouettes were barely visible against the fiery sun. Both men watched in awe at the beauty of the Nahanni and both men knew they would never see it again after this day.

They remained silent as the helicopter arrived and hovered above the clearing.

# Chapter 48

Word had spread quickly through the tiny town of Watson Lake and a crowd was beginning to gather in the parking lot of the RCMP station. An ambulance was on hand, along with two paramedics and supplies, to rush Erik Keller to the Whitehorse hospital three hours away. Ron Jenkins had shown up to help direct traffic and the team from the mountain search had already been transported back to the station.

Several town folks were on hand and even the eldest of them could not recall a survivor of a bush plane crash surviving two weeks, alone and exposed to the elements. Anita had arranged for meals to be delivered to the station for all of the officers and was patrolling the lot acting as the de facto 'homecoming director'.

There were over one hundred people there when the bush helicopter started its descent. Lauren Keller had a prime location near the front, Ron holding her hand so she didn't over excitedly rush the copter before it was finished landing.

Once the runners were on the pavement and the blades were slowly winding down, the door opened. Out came Peter, who helped Erik out and safely to the ground. Lauren couldn't believe the sight of her husband. He looked like he had lost forty pounds and aged ten years. He was dirty, bloody and hadn't bathed in weeks.

Still, she couldn't have loved him more.

Ron knew it was time and released Lauren from the safety of his grip. She took off on a dead run and did not stop until she was in the arms of the man she promised to love forever over twenty years ago. She squeezed him and her emotions overwhelmed her as she sobbed uncontrollably.

"It's alright, Honey. I'm here, I'm here. I love you," Erik quietly whispered in her ear.

At that precise moment, the crowd cut loose, as if on cue, and started to clap and cheer. There wasn't a dry eye in the house. Even the most seasoned officers were surprised by the emotion of the event. Peter and Lauren helped Erik to the ambulance where they laid him on a gurney. The two paramedics went to work fast, one taking blood pressure and the other hooking Erik up to an I.V. of saline.

"I told you... I always get my man, Mrs. Keller," Peter said, with a wry smile.

"Smartass," Lauren chirped as she pulled him tight. "Thank you so much, Peter. I will never forget this."

She could have sworn that she saw a tear in his eye.

Lauren gently kissed Erik on his swollen cracked lips. She took a step back and gave both Peter and Erik a quizzical look.

"What is that smell? Have you two been drinking??"

Both Erik and Peter began to laugh uncontrollably.

As the paramedics worked, the lovefest ensued. Lauren could not stop hugging and thanking everyone on sight, especially Ron with whom she had developed a father/daughter connection with. All of the Officers came by to congratulate Peter, even the Fort Laird team who had arrived in a separate helicopter shortly after the first.

"We have to get Erik moving," Peter announced to Lauren, amid the chaos. "Those were rented choppers and they can't make the trip to Whitehorse. They don't have the proper medical set up on board. Erik still needs serious care and this ambulance has to get moving."

That is when young Officer Marchont emerged from the crowd, and with him, he brought perhaps the most surprising news of the day.

"That ambulance isn't needed."

Peter and Lauren had looks of confusion on their faces as Marchont continued.

"Commander Emmerick heard about our discovery of Mr. Keller and ordered the Canadian Elite's own personal helicopter to aid in the rescue. It was not here in time for the evacuation but it's due here any minute and it sure can get Mr. Keller to Whitehorse a lot faster than an ambulance!"

"Well......how about that? Old Lucas Emmerick has a heart after all!" Peter exclaimed.

The festivities continued, Erik was even able to sit up and greet a few well-wishers, though Lauren and Peter were careful to keep too many people from crowding him. Even Winnie had made a new friend as Anita snuck her pieces of blueberry muffin when Peter wasn't looking. The town's fire whistle was roaring as a sign of celebration just as the CER chopper was landing.

Lauren, Peter and the two medics wheeled Erik to the door where the gurney was safely lifted into the bird. There were no goodbyes, the door closing quickly as the chopper started to lift. Lauren's face was in the window as they floated away.

The last thing Peter saw, she was waving and mouthing the words, 'Thank You.'

It well over an hour before the excitement dwindled and the crowd dispersed. The sun was low in the sky when Peter carried his pack over to his old pick-up truck and dropped the tailgate. He sat down upon it and pulled off his boots. Winnie jumped up and sat next to him and he put his arm around her neck and gave her a squeeze.

"Good days work, girl."

The two of them sat there for several moments

just breathing and being. It was only when Ron walked over that they broke back to the present. He had two cold bottles of Molson Canadian in his hands and he handed one to Peter. They both took long pulls from their bottles as they sat there.

"Enjoy it Peter. You and I both know that it doesn't usually end this way."

"I know, Ron......don't I know," Peter said, his voice drifting at the end.

"Well I'm going to get Winnie home and get myself a glass of scotch," he said as he handed the empty bottle back to Ron. He looked the grizzled old Lieutenant in the eyes and held out his hand.

"It's been an honor working with you, Sir."

Ron took his hand in a firm grip and gave him the nod of understanding that only two men who had been through it all would understand.

"It's been a pleasure serving with you, Sergeant," Ron said, and with that, he turned and walked off into the evening.

Peter hopped down from the tailgate and walked in his stocking feet to the driver's side door. He opened it and Winnie climbed in and took her usual spot in the passenger seat. Peter started the truck, pulled out of the parking lot, and started down the long dirt road home.

# Chapter 49

When the CER helicopter dropped them at the Whitehorse hospital a team of doctors was already on the tarmac to whisk Erik away. The story of the man who had survived a plane crash and two weeks in the freezing Nahanni was not even a day old, but already reporters from several different news agencies had swarmed upon the hospital.

Lauren was told she would be given updates as soon as there were any to give. She was shown to an office where she cleaned up. The boys were already en route, courtesy of one Ron Jenkins, who had personally arranged and paid for their flights. Marchont was able to get her a phone call home that morning and she had giddily informed the boys that Erik was alive and well.

The emotion of the call was too much for

Calvin. He had tried so hard to be the man he needed to be for Lauren and now the news of his father being alive turned him into a little boy again. He wept openly and told his mother that he loved her, which in turn made her cry.

Little Evan responded predictably, in his usual confident manner.

"I told you, Mom!!! I told you Dad was tough. He would never leave us alone, I told you."

She could not help but laugh at her little man.

Lauren washed her face, brushed her teeth and lay on a sofa in the office. It was her intent to rest her eyes for only a moment, but exhaustion got the better of her and she fell into a deep sleep. It was four hours later when Erik's doctor woke her. She quickly sat up and gathered herself and spoke.

"I'm so sorry, I didn't mean to be out so long," Lauren apologized.

"No worries, Ma'am. Your husband is doing alright. The infection in his blood was even worse than we thought, one more day and he couldn't have survived it. We have him on several different antibiotics and we expect improvement soon. We set his broken ankle as well. He is in surgery right now to place rods and pins in his wrist and hand. I'm afraid he is going to be looking at a few more surgeries and rehab to have full use of his hand again."

"Other than that is he out of the woods? A full recovery is expected?" Lauren inquired.

"I am happy to say that we foresee no complications. Your husband is a very lucky man. He will be out of surgery soon and you can see him in the recovery room."

"Thank you."

Lauren spent the next two hours on her phone contacting family members. She had regained cell service when she got to Whitehorse and felt connected to the world once again. Everyone was thrilled to hear about Erik's discovery and back home plans were already in the works for a huge celebration. She was so busy on the phone she almost didn't see her two boys standing before her.

"Hello??? Earth to Mom!!"

She looked up to see Evan standing in front of her, and Calvin right behind him.

"Boys!!" she screamed, leaping to her feet. The three of them combined for one huge embrace and each of them was overjoyed to see one another.

"How did you get here so fast?"

"Mom, we were on the plane in Syracuse by one PM. It is four in the morning now. We have been flying all day", Calvin stated.

"It's been such a crazy day, I just lost track of time. How did you get here from the airport?"

"C'mon, Mom, get with it. Calvin got us an Uber!!" Evan boasted.

She laughed aloud and hugged each of her boys again.

"Who wants to see Dad? He just got to the recovery room; I think we can see him now."

Lauren and the boys headed to the recovery room. Once there a friendly nurse went to check on Erik. A few minutes later she returned and told them they could enter the room. Lauren had warned the boys that he had suffered injuries and they must be quiet, calm and patient when they see him. As they entered the room they saw him for the first time. He had been cleaned up and his arm and leg were elevated and cast. His eyes were only partially opened and he was still under the effects of his anesthesia. Evan spoke first.

"Hey, Dad. I missed you. Did you see any bears?"

Erik's eyes opened a little wider and he let out a soft chuckle.

"Hi, my boy. See any bears?? Hell, I SHOT one that was trying to attack me."

"WHOAA!!!! Really? Awesome!!" wide-eyed Evan blurted out.

Erik looked at his oldest son.

"Calvin, come close son", Erik reached for his hand," I'm proud of you. Your mother told me how you stepped up and took care of things at home. I'm proud of you and I love you."

Calvin bent down and hugged his father, probably for the first time in ten years.

"I love you too, Dad."

The four of them spent the next several hours catching up as Erik shared some of the details of his adventure with his family. Only after a nurse chased them off did Lauren and the boys leave to get a hotel room.

It was several days before Erik was allowed to leave the hospital. His blood infection was gone and his bones were all set and ready to heal. The family had been minor celebrities in their short stay and everyone wanted to hear their story. The reserved Keller family declined all interviews, instead, asking that their privacy be respected.

Later that week the four of them were boarded on a small plane to begin the long trip home. The boys sat in front of Lauren and Erik as the plane left the ground. They were arguing over who would get the window seat on the next leg of their journey home. Normally this type of behavior would elicit an angry reaction from Erik, but this time he just laughed and shook his head. He vowed during his ordeal in the Nahanni that the little things would never bother him again.

Erik held Lauren's hand as she rested her blonde head on his shoulder. When the plane gained altitude and banked left he got what would turn out to be his last view of the Great Canadian North, for he never would visit the country again.

As he watched the beautiful mountains and lakes disappear into the distance he felt a calm come over him. He was going home with his family and for that he was thankful.

# Chapter 50

It had been well over a month since Peter and the rest of the RCMP Watson Lake detachment had saved Erik Keller from the Great Nahanni Park. They were all celebrated for a short time, the Canadian government had even doubled the station's budget, but everything had returned to normal. All of the Officers had returned to their regular schedules and the tiny town of Watson Lake had settled in for its long annual hibernation.

Peter McEwan, no longer Sergeant, drove his brand new pick-up truck into town, Winnie riding shotgun. It was the first new vehicle he had ever owned and he had purchased it last week on his last day of active duty. He had reached his twenty-five years, filed for his retirement and was on to new adventures.

His sister and nephews were thrilled that he had also purchased a nice little ranch home at the end of a cul-de-sac, four houses down from them in the Toronto suburbs. It had a fenced in back yard for Winnie and there was a dog park down the street where she could terrorize other dogs.

Peter was going back to 'Join the world of the living' again.

He had sold his cabin to the new Lieutenant who had been promoted to the Watson Lake detachment. The guy seemed nice enough and Peter hoped he could run a tight ship just like Ron Jenkins had. Old Ron had moved to the States, Boca Raton actually, and was living a life in the sun. He had recently discovered and learned how to use e-mail and sent Peter a message saying he was 'tired of sweating his ass off with a bunch of goddamn blue hairs down here on the equator'.

Peter laughed at that one for a long time.

Peter had a few loose ends to tie up before leaving town, say goodbye to some old friends and such. One of his last stops was the station. He pulled in and for an instant forgot that he wasn't there for work. He hopped out of the truck, Winnie on his heels, and entered the station.

"Well, look who can't stay away!"

It was Sergeant Marchont. Yes, the kid was so vital to the Keller case that orders came from the top to fast track his promotion.

"Don't worry, kid. I won't be here for long," laughed Peter," I just came to give you something."

He handed Marchont a binder full of folders.

"What's this?" asked the new Sergeant.

"Aw, this is just personal notes and observations on all of the search and rescue cases I've worked on in the last twenty-five years. There are six more boxes of these in the back storage room. They are all yours. If you ever need any advice I'm a phone call away. You're going to do great, kid. Congrats."

Peter stuck out his hand, but the young Sergeant did not shake it.

Instead, he stood straight, snapped to attention and saluted Peter. Upon seeing this, the other five officers in the station did the same. Peter felt a lump in his throat at this sign of respect.

"Thank you, men. You all are the best of Canada. Take care."

Peter turned and left the office before the men could see a lone tear roll down his cheek. He reached his truck, composed himself and drove to Anita's place. Once there, several local people shook his hand and wished him well as he bought a few meals for the road. Anita put such a bear hug on him he thought he might never break free. He paid for his meals, said his goodbyes and left.

Peter had shipped most of his personal belongings to his new home already and he and Winnie were traveling light. He needed only to stop at the post office and forward his mail before leaving town. Peter went into the office, filled out his change of address papers, grabbed his mail and hopped into his truck. He nearly drove off before an envelope caught his eye. The return address was from New York State. Peter opened the envelope and pulled out a letter and an airline ticket. He read the following:

*Dear Peter,*

*We hope you are well. Sgt. Marchont wrote to us of your retirement and the purchase of your new home. Congratulations. Things continue to get back to normal for us. We've had John's funeral and Erik continues to heal and hopes to return to work after the first of the year.*

*I have thought long and hard about what we owe you, how we can thank you, but nothing seems to be good enough. I only hope you know how thankful we are for the new lease on life you helped to give us. We are eternally thankful and if you and Winnie are ever in the area we would be insulted if you did not stop in to say 'Hello'.*

*Oh, Peter one last thing. Life is for the living and its time you get started. Maybe this airline ticket will be a good first step........*

*Eternally thankful, your friend,*
*Lauren Keller*

Peter pulled the ticket from the envelope. It was a round trip ticket, first-class from Toronto to Edinburgh, Scotland.

He smiled and looked at the ticket for a few moments. There were many memories he was leaving behind up here in the great white north, but his rescue of Erik Keller would end up being his favorite. It was like his sister, and Lauren, told him. You never know where life will end up taking you.

Peter put the letter and ticket into his glove compartment, put his truck in gear and pulled onto the highway. He kept looking in the rearview mirror until the small town of Watson Lake disappeared from sight.

"Let's get a move on, Win. It's a long way to Toronto."

Winnie hopped over to the passenger side window that Peter had rolled down for her. She stuck he head out and happily let her long ears flap in the breeze.

## THE END

Follow William A. Welsh (WA Welsh)
on Facebook
and
@randomguysbook
on Twitter


Please remember that the indie author depends on your reviews so please leave one on Amazon. Thank you!

Made in the USA
Middletown, DE
02 June 2020